AUTUMN ETERNAL

Autumn Eternal

KYLE BAGSBY

Yevhen Karpenko

Climb Hazard Pub

Autumn Eternal Copyright © 2018 by Kyle Bagsby. All Rights Reserved.

All rights reserved. No part of this book may be reproduced in any form or by any electronic or mechanical means including information storage and retrieval systems, without permission in writing from the author. The only exception is by a reviewer, who may quote short excerpts in a review.

Cover design and Illustrations by Yevhen Karpenko

This book is a work of fiction. Names, characters, places, and incidents either are products of the author's imagination or are used fictitiously. Any resemblance to actual persons, living or dead, events, or locales is entirely coincidental.

First Printing: May 2018
Second Edition: September 2024

CONTENTS

DEDICATION

For Mom,
Here's to hoping there are books in Heaven.
P.S. I miss you.

PREFACE

As cliché as it may sound, this story begins in the same way as many have before it. Once upon a time, a young boy, no older than three, was sent to live with his aunt and uncle halfway across the country. Partly fate, but mostly tragedy, led Kip to his new home. His parents had passed away after a horrible accident, and John and Susan were his only relatives. And no, the aunt and uncle are not evil, cruel, or anything of the sort. Actually, quite the opposite. The two run the general store on the corner of Elm Street and Patrice Avenue, in the sleepy little town of Arno, and love Kip as their own.

Arno is a town that can't be found on most maps. To get there, you take the gravel road off Highway 62 just before it ends. Then you cross two mountains, go through a valley, and then there's the river, which is rather tricky to traverse most of the year. After all of that, you follow the gravel road, and go about halfway through the forest and you're there. Can't miss it. Come to think of it... the chances of missing it are pretty high. Very few people ever leave, and the townsfolk get no more than one or two visitors a year.

And before you continue, there's one more thing you should know: it was eternally autumn in Arno. That would be the season between summer and winter, and the townsfolk never seemed to notice. Nonetheless, this story isn't as much about Arno and the seasons as it is about Kip and the adventures that await him.

~ 1 ~

WHERE BIRDS MOO

The soft light of the streetlamps drifted through the open window, still carrying the chill of a cool autumn night. Kip Carringer rolled a pencil, riddled with chew marks, between his fingers, lost in thought. It was Tuesday.

Kip was an average twelve-year-old boy, and about the least popular kid in school. Seventh grade was turning out to be much like the sixth grade for him: everyone thought he was different, and he often found himself awake before the rest of the town. Dawn was near, but Kip had been awake for hours. He raked his fingers through his shaggy brown hair, which had grown a bit too long, before going back to his drawing. Kip longed for something more, something beyond the confines of his current life. Above all, Kip realized, he needed a haircut.

The walls of his quaint little room were adorned with sketches of brave knights battling fiendish goblins, while dragons soared across the horizon. The floor was littered with books, journals, and papers that had spilled over from the cram-packed shelves. The breeze from the window ruffled his hair and sent a chill through his body, causing him to shiver before leaning back in his chair to stretch his arms and legs.

For a time, Kip gazed out the open window, watching the shadows dance. His aunt and uncle ran the general store in town, and the three lived in the loft above the shop. Wide-eyed, he stared into the darkness beyond his second-story window. The stone-paved streets were empty, but not for long. The autumn festival was starting, and everyone would soon be busy setting up. However, Kip wasn't a fan of the festivities; he found the whole ordeal redundant and couldn't understand why everyone was so excited. Pumpkin judging and hayrides were not his ideas of a good time.

The smell of simmering bacon brought him back from his thoughts. Kip closed his notebook and shut the open window, then grabbed his worn ball cap off the desk to hide his unruly hair and tucked the pencil behind his ear. A pleasant voice followed a soft knock at his door.

"Kip, are you up?" Aunt Susan's voice called.

"Yes, Aunt Susan," he responded.

"Would you be a dear and run downstairs to get us a loaf of bread?" she asked.

Kip opened the door. "Of course," he replied.

Susan leaned in and kissed his forehead. "Good morning." Her smile was ever-present, a smile that only she could conjure. Aunt Susan couldn't have children of her own and loved Kip more than anything. She had lived in

Arno her entire life, alongside her sister, who was Kip's mother. Kip's parents had met when his father, a lost salesman seeking directions, stumbled into the general store. They lived there together for a few years before marrying at the church down the street. Kip's mother was an adventurous woman, and his father vowed to show her the world. They moved away from the town, but Susan's sister always sent postcards from their travels. They had planned a trip back to Arno so Aunt Susan and Uncle John could meet their baby boy, Kip. That was just before the accident.

The wooden stairs creaked and moaned beneath Kip's feet as he ascended. He reached the shelves, grabbed a loaf of bread, and made his way back up the stairs. Aunt Susan thanked him for the bread and instructed him to sit.

"Breakfast will be ready in just a minute," she assured him.

"Did you write the bread in the ledger?" Uncle John inquired, peering over the newspaper.

"No, but I'll do it on my way out," Kip replied, pouring himself a glass of orange juice.

Uncle John ruffled the paper. "Are you looking forward to the autumn festivities, Kip? Maybe you can ask that pretty girl to the Harvest Ball. What's her name again?"

"It's Marleigh, Uncle John, and we're just friends," Kip clarified.

"That's the one. She is quite charming, Kip. Almost as pretty as your Aunt," Uncle John remarked with a sly smile.

"Oh, you stop that and eat your breakfast," Susan

scolded, balancing plates in her hands. She placed one in front of John and the other in front of Kip. "Eat up, honey."

The plate in front of Kip was more than full, with eggs, bacon, and a side of toast with butter. They always ate breakfast and dinner together, and Susan always packed Kip a homemade lunch. As they ate, they discussed the happenings of the town while the sun began to rise and chase off the night sky. Kip shoveled the last piece of bread in his mouth before collecting his things.

Hurrying out of the door and down the wooden steps, Kip avoided the second step from the bottom, which hardly counted as a step at all. It was a chilly autumn morning, but the breeze carried a certain warmth. The sun peeked over the roof of the store, casting shades of gold and red through the sky. Kip's bike leaned against the storefront. He slung his backpack over his shoulder and headed down the stone-paved street.

Arno was a peacefully crowded town nestled amidst a magnificent forest. Wood and stone houses lined the streets, leaning against one another in many places. Red and gold leaves adorned tree branches scattered through-out the quaint town.

Marleigh Belle lived roughly halfway between the general store and the school, making it convenient for Kip to meet her as she left her house. She resided in a brick house just a couple of dozen paces off Main Street. Kip could see the smoke curling into the morning air from her chimney as he turned off Elm Road. There she was, sitting on the front step, waiting for him, her blonde ponytail swaying in the cool breeze. Green eyes gazed towards him from behind square, black-framed glasses that were a little too big for her face. The two had been friends forever.

"Hey, Marleigh!" Kip exclaimed with a bright smile, hopping off his bike.

She replied with a sarcastic smirk. "Shut up, Kip."

"Why do you always have to be so hateful?" Kip exclaimed, shrugging with frustration.

"Because you're my best friend, and we're gonna be late again if you don't stop talking," she retorted as the first school bell echoed through Arno. "See!?" With the bike in tow, the two headed for school.

With autumn came the fall festival. The streets were lined with pumpkins, while hay bales sat around every street corner. Soon, there would be booths lining the streets, and vendors getting ready.

Kip watched as a gray bird on a lamppost ruffled its pale gray feathers and let out a somewhat exhausting "moo."

"I'll never get used to that," Kip lamented, hanging his head.

"Get used to what exactly? Birds doing what they're supposed to do?" Marleigh laughed.

Kip threw his arms in the air. "Birds aren't supposed to moo, they're supposed to chirp or squawk."

"Birds moo, Kip, get used to it."

"No, they don't! Every book I've ever read says they sing or chirp. Never a mention of mooing!" The subject always frustrated Kip and came up often. "So, what sound does a cow make?"

"They moo, of course. You know you're crazy, right?"

"I give up."

"Good." She just grinned at him and pushed her glasses up off her nose.

❊ ❊ ❊

The second hand on the clock seemed to drag more slowly than usual, agonizingly lurching forward one notch at a time. Kip stared at the clock until his vision blurred and his thoughts began to roam. Mr. Tinson's voice droned on about algorithms or some other nonsense. Kip pulled his sketch pad out from under his textbook and started drawing the outline of a new creature for the story he was writing.

He wrote the name "Squablin" underneath it. It was part squirrel and part goblin, but mostly goblin. Colored and covered in fur like a squirrel, but dumpy like a goblin. Kip outlined the bushy tail and cute little ears, then wrote a one-word description under the name: Mischievous.

The bell rang, and the usual commotion began. Gary Turner snatched Kip's drawing, and the typical game of keep-away ensued.

"Give it back, Turner!" Kip shouted.

"Let's see what you've been working on first, Kippy." Gary Turner flipped through the pages and announced the content for the whole class to hear. Laughter erupted as the details of Squablins were discussed mockingly.

Kip made a futile effort to retrieve the pad, held hostage behind Gary Turner's back, but he couldn't reach. Not that it would've done him much good if he could have.

"Don't be a bully, Gary," scolded Marleigh as she took the pad and handed it back to Kip.

"Better be glad you got saved by a girl, or you wouldn't get it back," Gary Turner laughed and sneered before leaving the classroom.

"Thanks, Marleigh."

"Well... someone has to look out for you," she grinned, flashing her usual smile.

There wasn't much beyond Arno, and the countryside remained mostly quiet except for the whir of a bike chain and the gentle click as it passed by each gear. The moo of a hawk could be heard overhead as well. Kip shook his head and did his best to clear his mind. Every day after school, he would follow the gravel road outside of town, venturing a little farther each time. He had to be back at the shop to help with the dinner crowd and to do his chores by six o'clock.

Taking a deep breath, Kip removed his feet from the pedals and let the bike coast. He wondered if there was something more out there than pumpkins and fall festivals. Tired of being picked on and pushed around, he longed to write his stories and draw, but it seemed that no one was content to leave him to his hobbies. Aunt Susan and Uncle John were kind, but he always felt out of place. Marleigh was his only friend.

Despite the warm weather and blue sky, the wind carried the chill of autumn, mingled with the scent of pine and smoke. Bringing the bike to a stop, Kip skidded in the gravel, sending little bits of rock scattering. He pondered the source of the smoke. There were no houses this far outside of town, and there was no reason for anything to be burning.

As the wind steadied, Kip observed smoke climbing and twisting from the cover of trees deep in the valley near the river. His mind raced. The townsfolk often spoke of the witch who used to live in the woods, but she was nothing more than a fond memory to most. This had to be her home, and he felt compelled to investigate, yet if he continued, he would be late. His aunt and uncle expected him to be punctual, and he always was. He didn't want to disappoint them, but he also yearned to explore.

Mulling over his options, he decided to wait until the next day. If he left straight from school and took the shortcut, he should have time to make it to the river and back before he had to be home. He gazed wistfully towards the rising smoke as the breeze caught hold of it and carried it off. Tomorrow.

Turning his bike around, Kip began to pedal.

❋ ❋ ❋

There was something peaceful about the sound of a broom dragging across a wooden floor that Kip found comforting. Sweeping the store floors was one of his responsibilities that he enjoyed. Kip often found that he came up with his best ideas while engaged in the simplest of tasks. He would conjure thoughts and run them through his head repeatedly until he could retreat to his room and put them on paper.

The store was rather small and getting crowded. Last year, Kip's Uncle John had made three wooden tables so they could serve meals. While Uncle John wanted to turn the place into a diner, Aunt Susan preferred to keep the store open as it was, so they compromised. They mostly served simple meals and sandwiches, which was enough to keep those three tables full.

"How was school today?" Susan asked Kip from behind the counter.

"It was good, Aunt Susan," he replied as he propped the broom in the corner and took off his apron.

"And how is Marleigh?" John inquired, rising from the table in the corner where he had been chatting with some of the townsfolk.

"I don't know, Uncle John. She's good, I guess." Kip may have been blushing a particular shade of red like that of a ripe apple.

"Did you ask her to the Harvest Ball yet?" Susan asked.

Kip was still beaming red. "No, ma'am."

"Maybe you should," Susan replied with a soft smile. "Would you mind running a delivery for me?"

"Yes, ma'am," replied Kip. Aunt Susan handed him a folded piece of paper and a brown paper sack for Elijah Winstead and sent him on his way. Kip tucked the folded piece of paper in his pocket and headed outside, making sure to avoid the second-to-last step that hardly counted as a step at all.

Mr. Winstead was elderly, and it was rare for him to leave his house. Most nights, Aunt Susan would send him something for dinner, and if Uncle John was busy, Kip would carry it. Mr. Winstead lived on Depot Street, nearly halfway between the general store and Marleigh's house. On nights like that one, Kip would follow Elm Road to Main Street and meet up with Marleigh before heading down Depot Street to Mr. Winstead's house. This way was well out of his way, but it was also well worth it.

As Kip passed by the town park and garden, laughter filled the air. Old and worn wooden fence posts leaned this way and that way, surrounding the park. Pumpkins and corn were grown in the garden, as nothing else would grow in Arno. The laughter was coming from Daisy Appleton, with Calvin O'Neal sitting next to her on one of the two little wooden benches in the park. Kip assumed Calvin O'Neal was the reason for her loud laughter, and perhaps he had said something charming or funny to her. The two were about to be married, and they were the talk of the town.

A little farther, Kip could see the quaint small brick house a couple of dozen paces off Main Street. Smoke curled into the night air from the chimney as he turned off Elm Road. Marleigh wasn't waiting on the porch for him. Kip went around the back of her house and searched for a pebble or small rock to throw at her window. He retrieved a smooth, polished stone next to the hackberry tree and rolled it between his fingers before hurling it at her second-story window. Unfortunately, Kip missed the window and struck the trim next to it.

Kip dusted his hands off and rubbed them against his trousers. He had felt something odd and reached into his pocket. Kip had forgotten about the note. He pulled it out but was struck by something on his head before he managed to open it. The stuffed teddy bear that hit him, now laying on the ground, had googly eyes that were too big for its head. One of the eyes was staring at Kip, and the other was staring off somewhere else.

"Oops," giggled Marleigh, leaning out of the window above him. "Guess my aim is better than yours!"

"Guess so," said Kip, rubbing his head.

"Whatcha doing out so late, Kip Carringer?" Marleigh asked.

"Just running something to Mr. Winstead," replied Kip.

"Want some company?" she asked from above.

"Yeah, if you want," Kip replied and picked up the teddy bear.

"Let me grab a sweater," Marleigh called to him as she disappeared back into her room.

Kip still had the folded piece of paper in his hand. He opened it carefully. There was only one word written inside: Courage. Aunt Susan would often give him notes of encouragement and praise. Usually, they were longer than one word and would say something like "you'll do great today" or "have the best day at school" or "don't give up." This note only said courage. Kip folded the slip of paper and shoved it back in his pocket.

The hackberry tree shook, and the leaves rustled as Marleigh began to carefully climb down one step at a time, just as she had done many times before. A moment later, she was on the ground smiling at Kip, a leaf was stuck in her hair, and Kip pulled it out.

"Here's your bear," said Kip, handing her the stuffed bear with googly eyes that were too big for its face.

"That's for you, Kip Carringer. You can keep it," Marleigh said, tightening her ponytail until she was content, and the two walked together toward Depot Street.

"I found something today," said Kip. "There's a house outside of town near the river. I saw smoke coming from the chimney. At least I think it's a house. No one lives out that far, so what could possibly be there? Maybe it's the witch."

"The witch?" Marleigh smirked. "She's been gone for years. Why do you think it's the witch's house?"

"I don't know, but what else could it be?" questioned Kip. "Will you go with me to find out?"

Marleigh pondered for a moment, and a sly grin crept onto her lips. "Maybe I will help you, Kip Carringer. Maybe I won't. Ask me again in the morning."

"But Marleigh," exclaimed Kip.

Marleigh shushed him and put a finger to his lips. "Ask in the morning, Kip Carringer." The two were standing outside of Mr. Winstead's house.

"Aren't you a little old for teddy bears, son?" Mr. Winstead muttered and laughed from his front porch. Most everything that came out of Mr. Winstead's mouth was nonsense or some kind of grumbling, but he always followed everything with a thick bellowing laugh. Kip thought it peculiar that Mr. Winstead was always amused by what he said and wondered if he would laugh at his own words when he was that age. Kip also thought it was peculiar that Mr. Winstead had precisely four teeth.

"Stop your lollygagging, boy, and bring me my sand-wich." There wasn't anything funny about what he said, but Mr. Winstead laughed his deep belly laugh regard-less. Kip hurried up the porch and handed him the brown paper sack, and Mr. Winstead thanked him and laughed once more.

Back in his room, Kip opened the window to let the cool night air inside. He placed the teddy bear with its big eyes on his desk and retrieved his sketch pad from his backpack. Tossing his ball cap onto the desk, he shook out his unruly hair while sifting through his drawings. Taking out some colored pencils, he began adding color to the Squablin. Using warm browns with a bit of orange accent here and there, he shaded the creature in. As he worked, he glanced up at the bear. One eye was looking at him, and the other was staring at the wall beside him.

Marleigh always liked his drawings, even though she laughed at a few of them. She would often tell him he was the best at drawing nerdy stuff and dragons, and he en-joyed what sounded like a compliment coming from her.

The house in the woods was on his mind as he drew. He wondered what and who could be inside. He thought about the stories he had heard of the witch who used to visit the village. He didn't know much, and people only mentioned her in passing. Oddly enough, only good things were said about her.

Shortly after, Susan came in. Kip was fast asleep. She

gently took the pencil out of his hand and set his drawing on his desk. Covering him with a thick quilt, she kissed his forehead one more time.

"Goodnight," she whispered.

WHERE KIP AND MARLEIGH
FIND A WITCH

Wednesday morning arrived just like any other, but for Kip, it held a heightened sense of excitement. Gathering his things in a hurry, he dashed out the door, skipping breakfast for once. Today, he wasn't dreading school. As he called out good wishes to his aunt and uncle, he hurriedly avoided the notorious second step from the bottom and made his way to Marleigh's house.

"Good morning, Mr. Belle," Kip greeted Marleigh's dad as he answered the door.

"Good morning, Kip," Mr. Belle replied with a warm smile. "Marleigh is in the living room."

Mr. Belle worked at the lumber mill and had been raising Marleigh on his own since her mother passed away when she was a little girl. Now, it was just the two of them living in the quaint brick house.

Entering the living room, Kip found Marleigh lying on

the wood floor, surrounded by markers and tubes of glitter, busily decorating a poster for the fall festival.

"Please, Marleigh," Kip began, hoping to capture her attention.

Marleigh smiled but remained focused on her task, tracing the outline of a rather large pumpkin with white glue.

"Marleigh, are you listening?" Kip persisted, despite her apparent distraction.

She finally looked up, a playful glint in her eye. "Please what?" she asked innocently.

"You already know what! The house in the woods. Will you go with me?" Kip inquired eagerly. "Aren't you excited?"

Marleigh let out a soft chuckle. "Yes, Kip, I'm positively brimming with excitement," she teased.

"Please, take it seriously," Kip pleaded earnestly. "No one lives out that far, so what could possibly be there? It has to be the witch."

Marleigh's smile widened as she looked up at him. "Oh, I'll take it seriously under one condition," she declared. "If you help me finish these posters." Holding out a marker to him, she added mischievously, "Ready to be covered in glitter?"

❋ ❋ ❋

The school day crawled by slowly, and Gary Turner only managed to steal Kip's ball cap once. Keep away never lost its appeal with his group, and they were adept at it.

Sometimes, Kip found himself wondering what it would be like if he were the bully, but one thing was certain: he wouldn't have relished picking on smaller kids.

There was a time when Kip Carringer and Gary Turner got along, they were even considered friends. They played baseball together on the same team when they were little. Gary was quite the athlete, even at such a young age, and Kip was almost a decent shortstop back then too.

When they were both five, they were friends, but by age six, they weren't. Kip wasn't entirely sure why; he just knew they weren't. Shortly afterward, Kip stopped playing baseball, and Gary stopped talking to him altogether.

Marleigh was always there to rescue Kip when he was in trouble, just as she was on that day. Kip felt a pang of sympathy for Gary Turner. He didn't entirely understand why he felt bad for him, but he did. When the final bell rang, Kip hurried to find Marleigh. The two gathered their bikes and headed down First Street before turning right onto Main Street, heading toward the outskirts of town.

"What's gotten into you today?" Marleigh asked as they pedaled steadily. "Hello, Earth to Kip?" He stared straight ahead as they rode.

"What do you think we'll find?" Kip questioned, the wind whipped around them.

"Not sure," she replied. "This is your adventure, not mine, and I'm really not sure why you're so excited about it."

"It's something different," said Kip. "And what if we find the witch?"

"Then we find a witch," replied Marleigh, shrugging in a casual manner.

Kip's gaze fixed on the distance. "We need to speed up though; I need to be home by six to help with the dinner crowd or I'll be in so much trouble."

"Kip Carringer, you've never been in trouble a day in your whole life," Marleigh giggled.

"It could happen," Kip said, not nearly as amused as Marleigh was.

The weather was cooler than the day before, and the clouds above hung low, colored a dreary gray. The air still smelled of pine, but the wind was stronger, the air heavier, as it usually was when rain was near. The gravel underneath them became rougher and more scattered as they ventured farther from Arno. These roads were rarely traveled.

From atop the highest hill, the two could see above the forest, spotting the river winding through the trees. They also noticed dark gray smoke climbing and twisting out from the cover of trees deep in the valley, near the river. Kip and Marleigh let their bikes coast down the slope, continuing on. They stopped at the bottom of the valley to survey their surroundings. The smoke emanated from deep in the trees, a good distance away from the road.

"Into the woods we go," said Marleigh with an optimistic smile.

Twigs snapped, and leaves crunched underneath their feet, adding to the symphony of forest sounds. Crickets chirped loudly and often, and a small owl had been following them for some time, leaping from branch to branch and mooing as it did so. The wind lingered between the trees, and fog began to rise as the pair went deeper and deeper into the woods.

Great oak and maple trees reached for the sky, and sunlight fell sparingly on the forest floor. The dense brush and thorny vines slowed their pace to a crawl, and both were covered in small cuts and scratches.

The forest abruptly ended, and the two tumbled out into the clearing. A messy little house stood before them as smoke curled from the chimney in puffs. It was pieced together with rough-cut lumber and bathed in dark green moss. Distressed burgundy paint still clung to the door, and a simple brass knocker was mounted in the middle. Kip cautiously stepped onto the porch, and the wood moaned and groaned beneath his feet.

Kip looked at Marleigh. "What should we do?" he asked in a hushed tone.

"This," she said, grabbing the door knocker and letting it fall. The thud seemed deafening in the quiet of the forest. Birds hurriedly scattered from their hiding spots.

After a brief pause, she turned the knob. "Looks like no one is home," said Marleigh. "After you." The hinges creaked as if they hadn't moved in a hundred years.

Kip stepped inside. The room he entered was small and dusty. There were windows on each side with the curtains drawn tightly, keeping all but a sliver of the afternoon light out. The air was damp and musty. His aunt would not be pleased that he was lurking about such a grim place, but she wouldn't find out about it either.

The breeze followed them in through the open door and made its way to the burning fire. The breeze and the fire swirled and played, sending embers floating throughout the room. Marleigh looked at Kip and winked before shouting, "Hello, any witches home!" Her voice echoed through the empty house.

Kip went wide-eyed before covering his face with his hands, peering at her through the slits between his fingers. "You're gonna get us cursed or something," whispered Kip.

"No, we'll be fine," she whispered back at him.

Shelves filled with trinkets and oddities lined the walls haphazardly. Jars of this and bottles of that sat here and there. Some were full of dead creatures floating in various liquids of various shades. A thick layer of dust and grime clung to everything. Kip picked up one of the jars and wiped the front clean. He shook it, and the contents began to glow a dull yellow. "Witch," he whispered to himself.

"Looks that way," said Marleigh, peering over his shoulder. "Where do you think she is though?"

"I don't know," said Kip.

Marleigh cleared the dust from the round wooden table in the center of the room. Symbols were carved into the wood, and she traced them with her finger. When she did, they began to glow softly. "These are stars and constellations," said Marleigh.

"What do you think is in there?" Kip pointed to the furthest wall. A thick blanket covered most of the door.

"Well, I guess we better find out." Marleigh pulled the blanket down; dust plumed around her. She opened the door, but it was too dark to see anything. She grabbed the jar out of Kip's hand and shook it. The light within grew brighter and brighter. She opened the jar, and a whirl of glowing specs spewed out like lightning bugs floating around the room. Two little white mice ran and dove for cover as they were startled by the light.

They both froze as they gazed into the room. A hooded figure's skull stared back at them. The skeletal frame, covered in a heavy wool blanket, sat slumped in an old leather chair. Bony fingers still clutched a rather large book clad in leather and bound shut with twine. A dozen or so withered sunflowers sat atop the book, bound with twine as well. Kip imagined them being a brilliant and bright yellow like they were when they were picked. They were not brilliant or bright anymore; they were dull and pale.

"I think we found the witch," said Marleigh.

"Yeah, I think you're right. What do you think happened to her?"

"I don't know," Marleigh paused. "She's just sitting there." Marleigh felt a pang of sorrow in her heart, and she felt sorry for the witch. "She's all alone."

Kip took a step closer as the light began to dim. He reached out and pulled the book from her grasp. The whole world seemed to go silent for a moment as he did.

"Do you really think that's a good idea?" asked Marleigh.

"No, but I want to find out what's in here," he replied as the light faded and the room went black again. "Let's get out of here." Kip stuffed the book in his backpack as the two headed for the door; Kip closed it behind them.

Outside, the temperature had dropped, and it was evident that daylight would soon give way to night. Marleigh and Kip went through the forest once again, retracing their steps. At the edge of the tree line, they retrieved their bikes and began the journey back to town. Kip's mind raced as he imagined what secrets the book might hold.

That evening, Kip swept the floors with purpose and rushed through his chores. He had intentions of skipping dinner, but his stomach had other plans. He hardly noticed the townsfolk's chatter or when Mr. Humphrey fell down the stairs outside. Everyone knew to avoid that second-to-the-last step. He finished up downstairs and grabbed a chunk of fresh bread before hurrying to his room.

Kip pulled the door shut and opened the window to let the night breeze inside. He removed the book and traced the leather spine with his fingers before setting it on the desk. The book was old and weathered, and the page edges were yellowed with age. He tossed his ball cap on the bed and retrieved a pocketknife to cut the twine that kept the book bound shut. His heart pounded in his chest, and his breath was rapid as he cut the twine and cracked open the book.

Blank. The first page was blank. The second was covered in random blotches of ink. The third was mostly the same, as was the fourth and the fifth, and all the numbers that came after. "How could there be nothing here?!" Kip said to himself, puzzled by what he saw as he turned the pages. This continued for the better part of half the book, and then it was back to nothing.

Disappointment lined his brow. All of that for nothing, he thought. He flipped through the book again until he came to the end of the ink-ridden pages. He pulled out his journal and set it on the desk. It wasn't a complete waste, though. After all, the book was rather nice and would be a fitting place for his writing and sketches.

On the first blank page, he began to draw one of his creatures, and under it, he wrote the name Squablin followed by "Mischievous."

~ 3 ~

WHERE MISCHIEF
STEALS PIE

Aunt Susan called from outside the door, following with her usual gentle knock. "Kip, are you awake?"

Kip jerked awake, drool still hanging from his lip. "Yeah, I'll be down in a minute Aunt Susan." He had fallen asleep with his face buried in his story. He had stayed up the entire night writing in his newfound book. Shuddering in the cold, he shut the window that had been open all night before raking his hands through his hair and reaching for his cap. Kip grabbed his journal and started towards the book before pausing. He decided against taking it with him, fearing that Gary Turner would get his grubby fingers on it.

"So, Kip, "said John, peering over his newspaper. "Have you asked that pretty girl to the Harvest Ball yet?"

"Not yet, Uncle John," he replied.

"You had better before someone else does."

Kip shrugged awkwardly, not knowing how to respond.

He sat at the table and took a drink of orange juice. "Can I get my breakfast to go, please?"

"Now, Kip, that's two days in a row. You know I like to eat as a family," said Aunt Susan with a disapproving scowl.

"I know. It's just been a busy week at school. I've been helping Marleigh with decorations," Kip explained.

John perked up at the mention of Marleigh's name. "Let him go, Susan. The boy has an important matter to attend to," he said, going back to his coffee, seemingly content with Kip's response.

"Okay, but tomorrow you're going to sit and eat," Susan said, handing him two brown paper bags, one with breakfast and one with lunch.

"Thanks, Aunt Susan," Kip said, kissing her cheek before making his way outside, avoiding the second-to-last step as always.

❋ ❋ ❋

Marleigh was grinning at him when he got near. She was sitting outside waiting for him. "Yesterday you were too early, and today you're late. Kip Carringer, you are becoming quite the rebel," she said, laughing.

"Aren't you even going to ask what was in the book?" exclaimed Kip.

"Wasn't planning on it, but I'm sure you'll just tell me anyway."

"Nothing," he said, pausing. "Absolutely nothing but ink stains and blank pages."

"Well, that's exciting," Marleigh said, smirking as they walked. The girl enjoyed nothing more than getting Kip worked up over anything.

"It's disappointing, that's what it..." Kip stopped on the sidewalk, stunned. Fuzzy brown ears stuck out from behind a shrub not ten paces in front of them. The creature wobbled out from its awful hiding spot before looking both ways. Satisfied with itself, the thing made a funny clicking sound into the air, and two more emerged from nearby. One fell from a tree with a thud, and the other rolled out from behind a bale of hay. Ears perked in unison as the little pack took off across the street and towards Mrs. Tubbertown's house.

Kip watched in awe as the three creatures stacked atop each other in the most uncoordinated fashion. The one on top stretched till his paws could reach the pie cooling in the window. They quickly tumbled down, pie and all, as the door slammed open and Mrs. Tubbertown emerged still in her nightgown and curlers with a broom chasing after them. The creatures bolted back across the road, tripping and falling over each other. Mrs. Tubbertown was winded, and her cheeks were stained a rosy shade by the time she made it to the street, ending the pursuit.

"Those are squablins...and they just stole a pie," Kip couldn't believe what he had seen.

"Yes, and it's Mrs. Tubbertown's stupid fault because she knows better than to leave a pie in the window. Although it is always funny to watch."

"What do you mean yes? Those are my squablins in real life!" Kip still hadn't moved.

"Kip, dear sweet Kip, we've already had the bird talk once this week. Do we really need to have the squablin talk too? We may need to get you checked out by a doctor. Think you're going a bit crazy if you know what I mean."

"No, Marleigh, I made them up, and I drew them," Kip said as he rummaged through his backpack for his sketch pad. "See, I drew them!" Kip flipped to the page where he had first drawn the picture.

"Congratulations on your accurate depiction of a squablin, Kip; however, they are usually a bit chunkier than that one. Still looks good though," said Marleigh with a grin. "We're gonna be late if we stand here all day." Marleigh grabbed Kip by the arm and started dragging him towards school.

❋ ❋ ❋

Never had a school day felt longer than that one. The usual classes and happenings seemed to drag on, leaving Kip lost in thought throughout the day. He pondered the possibility of the creatures being real, especially considering Marleigh's nonchalant reaction to them. Despite his confusion, he couldn't recall showing her the pictures he had drawn, which were still incomplete. What puzzled him even more was that it wasn't just Marleigh; classmates also made casual remarks about the creatures, as if they had always existed.

During math, Kip concluded that the morning's events must have been a dream. However, his confusion only deepened when, moments later, he witnessed two squablins hijacking a cart of pumpkins and racing down the road.

Until that day, Kip had never realized that a pumpkin cart could travel at such a high speed. The squablin at the helm clung to the wooden handle for dear life, its furry feet flailing in the wind like a flag in a storm. Meanwhile, the other squablin was likely buried beneath the pumpkins. The cart careened straight into Corey Randall's produce stand, sending pumpkins and corn flying in all directions. Despite his age, Corey Randall valiantly defended his stand until one of the squablins snatched his cane. Furious, he resorted to hurling ears of corn at them as they looted the place. Kip couldn't help but notice one of the squablins sticking its pink tongue out at the old man as they made their escape.

Kip went straight home after school. He had to make sense of what was going on. Kip considered going back to the witch's house, but it began to rain just as the school bell rang. Once again in his room, he studied the book over and over. Still, there was nothing. He sighed as thunder boomed in the distance. He wanted answers that just weren't there.

"Kip, honey," called Aunt Susan. "You have a visitor."

Kip wondered who would possibly be coming over to visit with him. He didn't have any friends. His answer came soon enough as the door swung open and Marleigh peered in. She looked more afraid of walking into his room than she did walking into the witch's house.

"So, this is where Kip Carringer hides out?" Marleigh

said, pushing her glasses up off her nose as she inspected the drawings on the wall. Her blonde ponytail bounced lively behind her as she walked.

"Why are you in my room?" Kip had a puzzled look on his face.

"Well, Kip Carringer, I wanted to check on my friend because I couldn't find you after school, and I wanted to see this book of yours that we risked life and limb to get."

Kip raked his hand through his unruly mess of hair and handed her the book. "Be my guest. There is nothing there till you get to my stuff in the middle." Lightning sparked the sky, and a clap of thunder followed close behind as the rain pittered and pattered against the roof.

Marleigh stood in the center of Kip's room and flipped through the pages. A puzzled look came over her face as she looked at Kip and then back to the book. She began to read aloud:

Summer is too hot, but winter is not, and spring isn't good for anything. Autumn is forgotten, but not for long. It is the only one that belongs.
-Lady Magdalene

"What are you talking about?" Kip studied her face, unsure of what to think.

"I'm reading, Kip. See?" She held the book out to him and pointed at the entry she had just read.

"Come on, Marleigh. It's just an ink stain. It doesn't say anything."

"Kip Carringer," Marleigh said, pointing at the page.

"These little things are called letters, and when you put them together, they make words... that you can read."

"But there's nothing there! Please don't joke right now," pleaded Kip.

"You really can't see it, can you?" Marleigh spoke candidly. Her expression showed both concern and confusion. Strangely enough, Kip was relieved. At least he knew she was not messing with him. She could see something that he could not.

"What else does it say?"

"Nothing else on this page, just some symbols and scribbles." Marleigh turned the page, mumbling to herself.

"Read it out loud," pleaded Kip. "What else is there?"

Marleigh began to speak and paused. She cocked her head, and a sly crooked grin started and spread from the corner of her lips. "Kip Carringer, do you know what today is?" The grin spread wider across her face as she spoke.

"Marleigh, please tell me what else it says. Please, please," he begged.

"Then you'd best play along if you want to know." She shut the book and folded her arms.

"It's Thursday," Kip replied reluctantly.

"Very good, Kip Carringer, and do you know what Saturday is?"

Kip swallowed hard. He knew very well what Saturday was. This particular Saturday was a day he dreaded on a seemingly regular basis. Every year during the autumn festival, the school put on a play. Kip was last featured in the play when he was six years old, and now it had nearly been a decade since that dreadful night when the cornstalk on stage left peed his pants in front of the whole town. Kip was that cornstalk, and not a single person in the town had forgotten the night that Kip Carringer peed his pants, even though his aunt and Uncle assured him that everyone would forget. They most definitely had not forgotten.

"Please don't make me do it." Kip looked like the saddest of puppies as his bottom lip curled under, and his eyes widened.

"Rehearsal is at 6:30, and don't be late. You get to be a cornstalk with me. They might even have your old costume still. I bet they even washed it." She winked and punched him in the arm before heading for the door. "Bring the book, and we'll look through it after practice."

❋ ❋ ❋

The rain had soon been reduced to a light mist, and a thick billowy fog had begun to flood the streets. Kip walked briskly along the stone-paved sidewalk, headed towards the school. Aunt Susan and Uncle John were most excited to let him have the night off for rehearsal. His aunt clapped with glee, and Kip couldn't be sure, but he thought he saw the beginning of a tear creep into the corner of Uncle John's eye.

Kip trudged along the sidewalk, kicking a pebble in front of him as he went, dreading the night ahead of him. He was in no hurry, and the streets were nearly empty. Come to think of it, they were completely empty. Before he knew why, the hair on his arms stood on end, and he could hear his own heartbeat in the silence. The streetlights dimmed, sending a chill through Kip's body. He felt as if someone was watching him. The eerie feeling wrapped around him as the fog closed in tighter.

"Is someone there?" Kip whispered into the dark, but there was no reply.

"Come out, Marleigh, I know it's you," he said with more confidence, but Marleigh wasn't there either.

Kip stood in silence for a moment, hearing his heart beating and the sound of his breath, and something else. It was a raspy sound, like a dried leaf being dragged across stone and then back again. It emanated from the alleyway between Elijah Winstead's house and the bakery.

Something was there, watching him. The space in the alley was full of fog, but something darker stood in the center. Something darker than darkness. Kip wanted to run, but he swallowed hard and held his ground. He stood his ground mostly because he was unsure if he could move his legs. The encounter lasted mere seconds but felt like an eternity. The darkness faded, and the fog took its place. Kip did his best to calm the drumming in his chest and jogged the rest of the way to school.

Hushed whispers erupted in the auditorium as Kip made his way inside, all while an overexcited cornstalk with a blonde ponytail and square, black-framed glasses waved joyfully at him from the stage. Kip hung his head as he made his way to the stage.

"Hey, Kip!" Gary Turner shouted from the front of the stage. "Make sure you don't pee yourself when I'm on stage. I don't need you stealing the spotlight from me again." Laughter and giggles filled the auditorium and echoed between the walls.

Kip could see Marleigh giving Gary Turner a piece of her mind, but he could not hear what she was saying over all the laughter. Gary just snarled back at her and returned to rehearsing his lines with Mrs. Karpinsky.

Kip found his costume and slipped it on over his clothes, making his way to the stage next to Marleigh. Her smile was soft, and she looked happy that he was there with her. Kip was relatively sure he was old enough not to pee his pants this year, but he still had reservations about being on stage.

For the next two hours, Kip swayed like a cornstalk should every time Liz Russell ran between him and Marleigh. Liz Russell was playing the role of the wind as she had for the past five years. Her brother Sam Russell was supposed to be playing the part of corn stalk number two, but he broke his ankle during a rather aggressive game of frisbee earlier that morning. Kip hadn't been aware that frisbee could be so dangerous and neither had Sam Russell.

The previous unfortunate event led Kip back into the role of corn stalk number two for the second time in his life. Apparently, he was rather good at it though because Mrs. Karpinsky had already applauded his realistic swaying and his ability to portray life in a corn stalk twice during rehearsal.

Kip's mind was elsewhere though. His thoughts were of the book and the secrets locked within. He wondered why Marleigh could see words and he could only see blots of ink. He wasn't wholly convinced that this wasn't an elaborate ruse just to get him back into the role of corn stalk number two.

He said the words she read over and over in his mind but couldn't make sense of them no matter how many times he repeated the passage. And then there was the shadow in the alleyway. Kip had decided to keep that to himself. No one would have believed him if he told, and he wasn't entirely sure there was anything there in the first place. Some things were better kept secret.

Kip hadn't noticed when Mrs. Karpinsky called the end of rehearsal, nor had he heard the dozens of pee jokes that were directed at him. He didn't realize rehearsal was over until Marleigh nudged him and told him it was time to go. She told him to meet her at the swings. So, Kip sat and waited on the swings with his feet dangling as his body rocked slowly forward and then back again.

"Hey, Kip Carringer." Kip could hear her soft smile without seeing her face. He wondered how girls could be so awesome and so mean all at the same time.

"Hey, you," replied Kip as he slipped down from the swing.

"Don't stop because of me," she said. "I was about to join you." Marleigh climbed onto the next swing over. "Did you bring the book?"

Kip nodded and pulled the old book from his backpack. He could still smell the witch's house in the leather bindings. He handed her the book.

"I read something earlier that has me thinking." Marleigh paused before continuing, "but you have to promise not to be all weird if I tell you what it says. I'm not sure I understand it anyway. Do you promise, Kip Carringer?" Her green eyes stared into his from behind her thick glasses.

"Yes," said Kip. "I promise."

The chains on the swing emitted soft squeaks and moans as Marleigh swayed back and forth, using her feet to propel herself. The sound carried through the night air, echoing across the empty playground. Squinting against the muted moonlight filtered through the fog, Marleigh scanned the pages of the book for a particular passage she had seen earlier.

Eventually, she found it:

I miss my home, and I miss my sisters, and I miss my cows, but I miss my Clarabelle most of all. Here in the woods, there are just birds that chirp and sing all day and all night. They sit on my window, and they whistle their songs, and they chirp, and they chirp, and they chirp. I wish that they would moo as my Clarabelle did, and then just maybe I wouldn't feel so alone.
- Lady Magdalene

Closing the book with a gentle thud, Marleigh handed it back to Kip. "What does it mean?"

"I made up the squablins. I drew their picture and wrote their story on these pages, and the next day they were alive," Kip explained, clutching the book tightly. "The witch wrote that birds should moo, and now they moo."

"And that Autumn is the only one that belongs. So, it is always Autumn," Marleigh added, pushing herself higher on the swing. The chains creaked louder, reaching further into the night. "Maybe you're not crazy after all, Kip Carringer."

"But why can't I read the book, and why didn't you believe me before?" Kip asked, puzzled.

Marleigh paused, pondering the question as the chill of the night wrapped around her. "Because you're not from here, and I am," she finally said, coming to a stop on the swings.

"What else is in here?" Kip held the book out to Marleigh.

Had Kip noticed the faint clicking sounds or the rustle of leaves nearby, he might have acted differently. But he didn't notice them, nor did he know what was about to happen next. As a result, he merely held out the book to Marleigh as a squat, fuzzy creature leaped through the air with determined eyes and grasping paws. It was part squirrel and part goblin, but mostly goblin. It was a squablin, and this particular squablin had a very bushy tail.

Kip lunged after the squablin, but it was too quick, disappearing into the fog with the book. Marleigh was almost certain she saw it stick its tongue out at Kip before vanishing.

Doubled over and breathless, Kip asked, "What do we do now?"

"The more important question is: what else did you write in that book, Kip Carringer?"

~ 4 ~

WHERE KIP BECOMES A HERO

As Kip stirred from his slumber, he felt an unusual weight pressing against his chest. It took a moment for him to fully wake up and realize that he was wearing something heavy. With a puzzled expression, he looked down to find a dull gleam reflecting off the metal breastplate he was wearing.

"What in the...?" he muttered, rubbing the sleep from his eyes. The straps of the breastplate were tangled around him, restricting his movements. He struggled to sit up.

Beside him, there was a dull thud as a dented helmet fell to the ground. Its visor was cracked open, as if it had been tossed aside in a hurry.

Kip blinked in confusion. "How did I...?"
The breastplate itself was worn and weathered, bear-ing the scars of past battles. Yet, amidst the scratches and dents, a simple cross caught his eye.

With a groan, Kip struggled to loosen the straps, his fingers fumbling in the dim light of dawn. Finally freeing himself from the armor's grasp, he couldn't shake the feeling of unease that settled over him.

"Why was I wearing armor in my sleep?" he wondered aloud, casting a wary glance around his room. He noticed a giant broadsword gleaming in the corner, the steel catching the early morning light, with a leather baldric laid on the floor next to it.

A voice came from the doorway, "Honey, you fell asleep in your armor again. That can't be comfortable at all. Hurry down before breakfast gets cold; you're eating at the table this morning." Aunt Susan picked up the helmet and set it on Kip's desk, then kissed his forehead before turning and heading back downstairs.

Kip sat down to breakfast in his armor and took a sip of orange juice. Armor was exhausting, but no one seemed to care that he was in it but him. Aunt Susan didn't mention it nor did Uncle John. They wanted to know all about the rehearsal and wanted to hear every detail of the previous night. He hung his head when he told them that he would be making his second appearance on stage as a corn stalk. Aunt Susan could hardly contain all her excitement.

"You best be headed to school, or you'll be late," said Aunt Susan as she cleared the table and Uncle John returned to his morning newspaper.

Kip gathered his things as best he could and headed outside in a suit of plate armor making sure to avoid the second from the last step that hardly counted as a step at all. Riding his bike to school was not an option on that day so he headed out on foot.

Marleigh was waiting for him impatiently with her arms crossed and tapping her foot against the pavers. "You're late, Kip Carringer."

"You're not going to laugh at me for wearing armor?" questioned Kip.

"Why would I laugh at you for that? Looking goofy in armor should be the least of your worries."

"But it's not real... well maybe it's real!? Real or not I wrote it in the book, and today I woke up wearing this!" Kip motioned to the shiny plate armor.

"What book?" Marleigh looked quite confused.

"What do you mean what book!" exclaimed Kip. He would have thrown his arms up in frustration, but his new attire made that exhausting and challenging.

"I mean, what book are you talking about, Kip Carringer?" replied Marleigh.

Kip was getting increasingly frustrated, and it was beginning to show. His ears turned red, and he clenched his fists until his knuckles turned white. It wasn't until then that Marleigh winked at him. Then she laughed at him.

"So, what exactly did you write in that book?" she asked.

Kip hung his head as low as he could. He was embarrassed, and he clearly didn't want to answer her question. "I wrote that I was the hero of Arno."

❈ ❈ ❈

Kip Carringer was greeted at school that day with a slow clap, leading into a standing ovation. He was somewhat sure the entire school was outside, waiting for him to arrive. Banners with his likeness hung next to the autumn festival decorations. Gary Turner emerged from the crowd and stood next to Kip. He put one arm around Kip and motioned to the crowd for silence before speaking.

"Good people of Arno," Gary Turner spoke with a smile etched on his lips. "I present you with our hero!"

Kip wasn't entirely sure what was happening, but he wasn't surprised at what did happen. The whole school had a good laugh at his expense. He was a joke before and remained a joke now. The only difference was the shiny suit of armor he wore that gleamed in the sunlight as he stood there.

Mr. Tinson showed up before long and ordered everyone to class, but not before catching a glimpse of Kip. The math teacher did his best to hide his amusement, but even his best attempt wasn't all that great. A moment later, it was just Marleigh and Kip standing outside of the school.

Marleigh smiled her usual smile as she turned to Kip. "Hey, look on the bright side, Kip Carringer. At least no one can shove you in a locker today. You won't fit!" She couldn't help but laugh at her own joke as she tapped on Kip's clunky armor. She took his arm, and the two walked into school together.

Simple tasks became a challenge that day. Sitting at a desk was no longer just sitting at a desk. It was a complicated procedure that required skill and forethought. Careful consideration was a necessity, and the constant pointing and laughing was no help. Kip just wanted to be out of the armor, and he wanted everything to go back to normal. Marleigh had pledged to help him get out of the metal suit, but they had to wait until lunch before they could sneak away.

On the bright side, Kip had not been stuffed into any lockers. He did spend the better part of gym class trying to figure out how to stand up after Gary Turner tripped him during dodgeball. Dodgeball would have been worse though if he didn't have the armor. When the lunch bell rang, Kip stayed behind in the gym. Marleigh was going to meet him there.

"Kip Carringer, you smell like a sock." Kip was sitting on the floor as Marleigh braced her feet against his waist. She had her arms wrapped around the breastplate and was doing her best to pull the thing up and over his head. Getting the armor off would have been much simpler if it had been properly fitted, and if it hadn't weighed so much.

Kip's hair was damp with sweat when they finally managed to remove the last piece. The two lay on the gym floor exhausted. "What if I wake up wearing it again?" Kip asked.

"If that happens, you better find a new friend." Marleigh pushed herself up and extended a hand to Kip.

"I think we need to find the book," said Kip.

"I think we need to learn how to track squablins first," mused Marleigh. "When you wrote about them, did you give them a home?"

"No, I hadn't got that far yet. Maybe we could go back to the park and see if that one shows up again."

"That sounds like fun," Marleigh said as she helped Kip get up and on his feet. "We can go back after rehearsal and stake out the place."

"We have practice again tonight?" Kip already knew the answer, but he asked anyway.

"Yes, Kip Carringer, we have practice tonight."

❋ ❋ ❋

"Oh, Lady Magdalene, where have you gone?" Gary Turner bellowed to the empty seats below, with longing in his voice. Well, they were mostly empty, aside from the seat occupied by Sam Russell, who spent the better part of practice mean-mugging Kip for taking his role of corn stalk number two. When Sam Russell wasn't mean-mugging Kip, he was drumming on his crutches in the most annoying fashion.

"Cue the wind," called Mrs. Karpinsky from offstage. Liz Russell skittered from behind the silky blue curtain and blustered between Kip and Marleigh, huffing and puffing as she went. The two dressed as corn stalks rustled and swayed as she passed by them. Mrs. Karpinsky did not look pleased, though, as she walked out on the stage.

"Mr. Carringer, the mood we're looking for is melancholy. You should appear sorrowful and desolate as the wind rustles you. You look like a rather cheerful corn stalk, and that just won't do. In act three, the witch has left us, and the mood of the town is not a cheerful one," Mrs. Karpinsky clasped her hands together behind her back as she stalked around the stage.

"Look at Mr. Turner, would you?" She motioned to Gary Turner, who was standing downstage center with his arms stretched out as if he was reaching longingly for something only he could see. He hadn't moved since he said his last line. "That is melancholy, Mr. Carringer. I'll expect better from you tomorrow night."

"Yes ma'am," replied Kip as he glanced towards his shoes.

"Yeah, hero boy, be more like me," scoffed Gary Turner.

"That's enough for tonight," said Mrs. Karpinsky as she addressed the room. "Rest up, and we'll see everyone back here tomorrow evening at 6:45 sharp." She dismissed the group and retreated backstage.

"Well, if it's any consolation, I thought you did great tonight," Marleigh said, flashing her usual smile.

"Thanks, just not sure how well I can pull off melancholy corn stalk," Kip replied, pulling the costume over his head and letting it fall in a heap on the ground.

"Oh, Kip Carringer, it's easy. Just think of something sad and do what I do," Marleigh said, her expression dimming just before she crossed her eyes and stuck her tongue out at him.

Kip had a hard time keeping a straight face, and his solemn expression quickly turned cheery. Marleigh had a way of always making him feel better, even when he didn't want to.

"So, back to the park tonight?" Marleigh asked.

"Yeah. Hopefully, those squablins will show up, and we can get the book back. Think I'm gonna try burning it," Kip replied.

"Does Kip Carringer not want to be the hero of Arno anymore?" Marleigh teased, her voice tinged with sarcasm.

"No, Kip Carringer does not," Kip answered.

The moonlight shimmered through the fog that night, casting a bright glow over the playground. Above, the stars twinkled and danced in the velvety expanse of the night sky. Perched atop a metal horse, Kip surveyed his surroundings. The once vibrant brown paint on the handle had faded, revealing patches of bare metal beneath. Despite its weathered appearance, the metal gleamed softly in the moonlight, polished smooth by countless hands over the years. Beneath him, the rusted spring groaned under his weight, a relic of childhood days long past.

Marleigh's gaze was fixed on the sky, lying in the grass a few steps away from Kip. "What do you think happened to the witch? I can't stop thinking about her being there all alone. That's just horrible," Marleigh lamented, her eyes still focused upward.

"I don't know. Maybe we could find out if we had the book," replied Kip.

"You know that book is some serious dark magic, right!? Everyone says Lady Magdalene was nice and pleasant, and nice and pleasant people don't just disappear only to be found decades later dead and holding a magic squablin-making book," Marleigh sighed.

"I saw something yesterday before practice," said Kip as he dismounted the toy horse. "At least I think I saw something."

"What was it?" Marleigh asked, her eyes widening.

"I'm not sure. It might have just been a shadow in the fog, but it felt like something was there."

"Probably just you being a scaredy-cat, Kip Carringer," Marleigh grinned up at Kip.

"Yeah, probably," he replied.

Kip wasn't sure if he had seen something the night before or if he was, in fact, just a scaredy-cat. Either scenario could have been true. The whole ordeal did make him wonder, though. Maybe there was something there in the alleyway between the bakery and Elijah Winstead's house, or maybe there wasn't.

Marleigh and Kip waited, but no squablins ever showed, and honestly, Kip wasn't entirely sure what he would have done had a squablin shown its furry little face at the playground that night. The two watched the stars for a while longer, paying special attention to one that twinkled in the night sky, shining just a bit brighter than all the rest. They stayed for a time before taking First Street to Main Street and then to Marleigh's house. On the way there, they passed townsfolk setting up booths and games for the coming festival. That night, Marleigh went in the front door instead of climbing the hackberry tree to her window, as she often did. She pondered about the witch, about Kip, and about the Harvest Play and Ball.

Meanwhile, Kip climbed the stairs to the general store, making sure to avoid the second from the last step that hardly counted as a step at all. Aunt Susan and Uncle John greeted him warmly, eager to hear how practice for the Harvest Play went. As usual, Uncle John asked about

Marleigh, causing Kip to blush a very deep shade of red. After that, Aunt Susan insisted he eat a sandwich, even though he wasn't hungry, before Kip retired to his room.

Inside his room, Kip pondered about the witch and about Marleigh. When he was nearly done pondering, he thought about the Harvest Play and the Harvest Ball, and then he thought about Marleigh some more.

$$\sim 5 \sim$$

WHERE SHADOWS EMERGE

That Saturday morning, Gary Turner slung his ball bag over his left shoulder and stepped out into the clear, blue morning air with a baseball in his hand. He threw the ball skyward, catching it skillfully before making a swinging motion with his hands, repeating the action in a practiced rhythm. "It's a line drive," he announced to the empty yard, "the shortstop reached for it, but missed by inches! It's all the way to the fence! Turner will turn this into a double! The crowd goes wild!" Running imaginary bases, he tore up the grass, sending the morning dew spiraling behind him with each step.

He tossed the ball into the air once more, but his attention was drawn to a raspy sound nearby. It resembled the noise of a dried leaf being dragged across stone, and it sent a shiver down his spine. The ball thudded on the grass a few feet away, rolling to the sidewalk, leaving a trail in the morning dew. Gary Turner didn't notice the ball, but he did notice the shadow watching him.

✽ ✽ ✽

Kip woke up that morning without his armor. He was thankful that at least one thing went his way; however, the gleaming broadsword still loomed in the corner of his room. Kip sat up, stretched, and yawned. The early morning sun beamed through his window, warming the room. He opened the window to let some fresh air in, and a breeze gusted in, toppling over the teddy bear with googly eyes on his desk. One eye stared at Kip, and the other glanced toward the wooden floor.

Thoughts of the book filled his mind. He had only had it for such a short time, and he couldn't remember everything he had written in it. Regardless, he needed to get it back to stop anything else from happening and to find answers to what was already happening. He wondered if the book was really the reason why birds didn't chirp or why it was always autumn.

The alluring aroma of simmering bacon brought Kip back from his thoughts. During breakfast, Aunt Susan and Uncle John were brimming with joy as they went on and on about how proud they were of Kip and how they absolutely couldn't wait to see him perform in the play that evening. Kip didn't share their enthusiasm, but he was in high spirits and looking forward to the day's festivities, especially sharing them with Marleigh. After breakfast, Uncle John slipped Kip some pocket money and with a sly wink told him to buy Marleigh something nice.

The town bustled with life and color. Arno's streets

were adorned with banners in bold shades of yellow, orange, and purple, casting a festive atmosphere. Grown-up townsfolk leisurely browsed from stand to stand, sampling spiced cakes and herbal teas, while children dashed from game to game, stopping only at stands offering sugary treats. Kip waited near the corner of Depot and Main, hands in his pockets, listening to the sounds of stringed instruments and drums carried along on the warm breeze.

"You could always browse while you wait," suggested Daisy Appleton, leaning against the wooden table. Darling bracelets and charming rings were neatly spread in front of her, and delightful necklaces dangled from strands of twine.

"Who says I'm waiting for something?" Kip asked as he picked up and looked over a silver bracelet laden with glossy stones.

"Boys are always waiting for something," Daisy replied, her smile soft and warm, making Kip blush. He wasn't accustomed to attention from pretty girls, and Daisy Appleton was much more than just a pretty girl.

"If I was waiting for someone and I wanted to get them a gift..." Kip paused nervously. "What should I get them?"

"Something special and something shiny," Daisy said. She knelt and opened the chest under the table, producing a little tiara that sparkled in the early morning light. She pulled a handkerchief from her pocket, licked the corner, and buffed out a smudge, then held it out for Kip to see.

"She'll like this?" Kip obviously knew nothing of girls and what they liked or disliked, for that matter.

"Yes, Kip, she'll love it," Daisy assured him. She handed

Kip the tiara, and he retrieved the money from his pocket that Uncle John had given him.

"How much is it?" he asked.

"That tiara is special, and no amount of money can buy it."

Kip looked puzzled. "Then what would you like for it?"

"That tiara will cost you a kiss," Daisy said, pointing to her cheek.

Kip blushed deeply, his palms beginning to sweat as he leaned in to kiss Daisy's cheek. When he opened his eyes, her smile was somehow softer and warmer than before. He thanked her, and she thanked him, and if it would not have drawn attention, Kip would have run away and hid.

Kip wandered into the town park, trying his very best to collect his thoughts amidst the music and dancing. He noticed the ever-so-handsome Calvin O'Neal, arm in arm with old Mrs. Tubbertown, skipping and dancing with joy. Surprised by Mrs. Tubbertown's happiness, Kip wondered if Calvin O'Neal would be jealous that he had kissed his fiancée on the cheek. Calvin O'Neal would not have been jealous.

A gentle tap on his shoulder made Kip spin around to find Marleigh. Her blonde hair was loosely tied with a bow, and an orange lily adorned her left ear. "Is that for me?" she asked, noticing the tiara in Kip's hand.

Kip, still clutching the tiara, nodded in response. Marleigh graciously accepted the shiny tiara and pinned it in her hair. "This looks like something a princess would wear," she smiled.

"That looks like fun," Marleigh remarked as she observed the crowd.

"What does?" Kip inquired.

"Dancing."

"But I don't know how!" Kip's face contorted with pure terror.

"Kip Carringer, don't tell me you're going to make a princess lead herself in a dance," Marleigh teased, her expression playful as she grabbed Kip's hand and pulled him into the park.

The music filled the air, lively and enchanting, as Kip did his best not to step on Marleigh's toes. They swayed, moved, and spun around in a dance that might have been a waltz or perhaps a samba, but it didn't matter because they were doing it all wrong. However, they were having an extremely good time doing so. The lute player shouted "vivace," and Kip assumed it meant faster, as the musicians sped up, and so did their dance. Right foot back, left foot back. Marleigh's laughter rang out, infectious, and Kip couldn't help but join in. When the song finally ended, they both collapsed onto the inviting grass, panting heavily, yet still laughing.

Nearby, Corey Randall called out to passersby, inviting them to guess the weight of the squablin inside the makeshift corral he had created. "Step up and guess its weight, and if you're right, you'll be the proud owner of your very own pet squablin! Only one coin to guess!" The squablin inside the corral was not pleased with its situation, furiously chewing at the leather collar and leash that kept it restrained.

"We need to free that squablin, Kip Carringer. It looks so sad on a leash," remarked Marleigh, her eyes fixed on the corral.

Kip fished a coin from his pocket and held it out. "Do you want to guess, or should I?" he asked.

"Either way, we're going to free that fuzzy little guy."

Corey Randall, sporting a red bowler hat that leaned to one side, stood nearby, his breath carrying the scent of radishes. "A single coin and it can be all yours, boy!" he boomed, his thumbs hooked around his tan suspenders.

Kip handed over the coin and pondered the weight of the squablin. It was about the size of a dog, but he wasn't sure how much a dog weighed. Corey Randall's patience wore thin, and Kip hazarded a guess. "Twenty-two pounds?"

Corey Randall leaned on his cane and chuckled. "Close,

but not close enough, son. Better luck next time." His laughter tapered off abruptly when the gate to the corral swung open with a loud crash, meeting the wooden post. Marleigh stood behind the gate, a sly grin on her lips. The squablin scrambled through the open gate, and Corey Randall leaped after it, grabbing hold of the leash.

Unbeknownst to the townsfolk at the time, Corey Randall would not return to Arno for about two weeks. The squablin, filled with pent-up energy, dragged him through the forest, across the river, through the valley, and most of the way up a mountain before finally chewing through the remainder of the leash and darting off. Corey Randall, in a foul mood, faced an adventure of his own trying to find his way back home—a tale for another time.

The day unfolded, and the festival continued with the sun hanging high in the sky, a perfect circle of golden warmth suspended in the blue expanse above. Kip and Marleigh reveled in games and treats, joining the town in its joyful buzz.

Later, as exhaustion began to set in, Kip escorted Marleigh to the general store, cautioning her to avoid the second-from-the-bottom step. Daisy Appleton winked at Kip upon their arrival, while Calvin O'Neal and Uncle John were engrossed in the newspaper. Aunt Susan emerged from the kitchen upon hearing the door.

"Have you kids had fun today?" Aunt Susan inquired.

"Yes, ma'am, today has been amazing!" Marleigh exclaimed, her shiny tiara slightly askew and the lily no longer neatly tucked behind her ear.

Aunt Susan adjusted the tiara and flower with a smile. "I'm glad. Are you two hungry?"

"Very!" Kip and Marleigh chimed in unison, sharing a laugh afterward.

"Good, I'll make you both something to eat, and you need to rest up before the play," Aunt Susan directed, motioning toward two empty chairs by the corner table. After bringing them cold glasses of tea, she retreated to the kitchen.

"Maybe being a cornstalk won't be so bad," Kip mused before taking a long drink.

"It won't be that bad at all, Kip Carringer," Marleigh reassured him.

Aunt Susan later brought them sandwiches and chips, leaving a sandwich on the back step for the squablin that had befriended her. She had found the creature injured in an alleyway, nursed it back to health, and grown fond of it.

Shortly after, Mrs. Karpinsky entered, looking disheveled. "Have you two seen Mr. Turner today? His mother said he caught the shadow this morning and wasn't feeling well," she expressed with concern. "I hope he's well enough; we need him tonight."

Marleigh furrowed her brow in thought. "No, ma'am, come to think of it, we haven't."

"Well, if you do, tell him I'm worried about him," Mrs. Karpinsky requested before leaving. Kip and Marleigh exchanged glances.

"Should we go check on him?" Kip proposed.

"I think so. It's almost time to go to the school," Marleigh agreed.

* * *

Kip stopped to retrieve the baseball that had rolled near the street, its worn red stitches familiar in his hand. The sun hung low, casting hues of gold and red across the evening sky as lively music filled the air, signaling the festival's continuation.

Marleigh rapped on the door, waiting patiently as sounds of scuffling emanated from inside. Mrs. Turner appeared, offering warm greetings. "Hello, Marleigh, and it's so good to see you, Kip. You never come around anymore. How are you two doing today?"

"We're good. Is Gary home? Mrs. Karpinsky said he wasn't feeling well," Kip inquired.

"Oh, honey, he'll be okay. He's just a shadow. He's in his room if you two want to say hello," Mrs. Turner reassured them.

Exchanging glances, Kip and Marleigh stepped inside. The house was quiet as they made their way down the hall. Kip hadn't been in Gary's room since they were children. Memories flooded back of sorting through baseball trading cards, building pillow forts, and crafting tin foil swords to fend off imaginary foes.

Pushing open the door, it creaked on its hinges. Gary lay motionless on the bed, his eyes tightly shut. A shadow enveloped him, its darkness seeming to ebb and flow over his body like black waters clinging to a sinking ship.

"Gary?" Kip called out, but there was no response. He crossed the room and placed a hand on Gary's arm, feeling the chill that sent a shiver down his spine. "What happened to him?" Kip turned to Marleigh, concern etched on his face.

"He's a shadow," Marleigh responded gravely. "But this isn't normal, is it?"

"No, I don't think so," Kip said, his voice tinged with worry. He sat beside Gary on the bed, with Marleigh joining him.

"I know I didn't write anything like this in there. I don't know... but it has to have something to do with that stupid book," Kip remarked, frustration evident in his voice.

"I know something is wrong, but it feels normal. I don't know how to explain it," Marleigh responded, her expression a mix of confusion and concern.

"We'll figure out how to make this right. We need to find that book, no matter what," Kip asserted, determination in his tone.

"We have to go to the school first," said Marleigh. "Mrs. Karpinsky will be looking for us. I don't think there's anything else we can do here right now." With that, Marleigh stood up and headed for the door.

Kip lingered behind, his gaze fixed on Gary's still form. "I'm sorry, Gary. I didn't mean for this to happen." As he followed after Marleigh, the darkness around Gary seemed to stir, lazily churning and spreading. It seeped into the wooden floor, climbing the walls and engulfing the room in inky blackness, covering the window and curtains in its eerie embrace.

❋ ❋ ❋

"Five minutes till curtain, the show is about to begin," called Mrs. Karpinsky with her hand cupped around her mouth. "Places everyone!" she clapped and shuffled through the papers of her clipboard, then repeated the action twice more.

Kip stood center stage. His palms were sweating, and his pulse was racing. He glanced back at Marleigh, who gave him an exaggerated wink. Since Gary Turner couldn't perform, Mrs. Karpinsky decided that Kip would have to fill in as the leading role. Sam Russell took Kip's place as corn stalk number two, wearing only part of the costume so he could still use his crutches. Kip tried his best to avoid eye contact, as Sam Russell continued to give him hostile looks.

Mostly everyone present would agree that the next hour and forty-five minutes were a complete disaster. The play consisted of three acts. The first was about the founding of Arno. The second was about the witch and all the good she did for the town, and the third act was also about the witch and her sudden disappearance, never to be seen again.

Everything went smoothly for about the first five minutes, and Kip was actually beginning to enjoy himself. However, the trouble started when Kip, wearing a costume tailored for Gary Turner, who was significantly bigger than him, attempted to jog offstage for a scene change at about six minutes into the play. Instead of heading to the backstage, Kip ended up tripping and rolling off the front of the stage, narrowly avoiding landing in Calvin O'Neal's lap. To add to the embarrassment, his pants remained onstage.

In the second act, disaster struck when a fire broke out, engulfing the cardboard school set. Initially, no one knew what caused the fire. Later investigations revealed that a disgruntled squablin might have been responsible or at least the prime suspect. This particular squablin had developed a craving for apple pie, which was among the snacks backstage. The enticing aroma must have lured the furry creature inside.

The only obstacle between the squablin and the apple pie was Betty Cordova, also known as Big Betty. Big Betty was known for her strength and dominance; she was always the first pick for dodgeball, and she once defeated Gary Turner in an arm-wrestling match, with Gary conveniently claiming to be sick that day. Gary was not sick that day.

It quickly became apparent that Big Betty wanted that pie just as much as the squablin did, igniting an intense battle. Costumes were ripped to shreds, and tables turned into scraps of wood and splinters. The play came to a halt as the audience froze, listening to the chaos unfold. Somehow, the cardboard school set, on wheels, was set ablaze and pushed onto the stage. In the end, Big Betty emerged victorious, savoring the sweet taste of victory in the form of that apple pie.

Finally, act three commenced, albeit with delays as everyone was brought back into the auditorium after being evacuated due to the smoke. The stage remained wet, and when Mrs. Karpinsky queued the wind, chaos ensued. Liz

Russell ran out, slipped, fell on her face, and slid into the cornstalks, while Marleigh fell on her bottom, laughing hysterically. Meanwhile, Sam Russell hobbled offstage, crying, and never returned.

When it was all over, the cast and crew took a bow, only for the curtain to fall on top of them. Those who remained in the audience, those who hadn't fled in fear, laughed, clapped, and cheered.

Kip and Marleigh stayed late to help clean up and console Mrs. Karpinsky, who vowed never to produce another play. Once the wreckage was cleared, they headed home.

"Well, that was a disaster," remarked Kip.

"Yeah, but at least you didn't pee your pants this time," Marleigh teased.

"Yes, Marleigh. At least I didn't pee my pants. As if that was going to happen again."

"You never know, Kip Carringer. You gotta go when you gotta go, and little Kip Carringer had to go while he was on stage in front of the whole town."

"Thanks for reminding me," Kip replied, rolling his eyes.

"Any time, best friend!" Marleigh winked her usual wink and punched Kip on the shoulder as they walked down First Street.

"You think Mrs. Karpinsky will be alright?" asked Marleigh.

"Yeah, but she might need some therapy."

"Maybe next year you can be a corn stalk with me, and Sam Russell can try out for the lead. Hopefully, he'll be walking by then."

"There's no way you're talking me into going through that again!"

"Even if we tie your pants up so they can't fall down? Or we could get you a really nice pair of suspenders. I know a guy."

"Remind me why we're friends again?"

"Because I'm awesome and your best friend, and you would be so lost without me," said Marleigh.

"If you say so."

"We'll figure it out, together."

"I like that plan," said Kip.

The two rounded the corner and turned onto Main Street. Crickets chirped and sang as they went, and an owl mooed at them from atop a lamp post. Kip and Marleigh crossed into her yard and stopped by the hackberry tree.

"And Kip, I thought you should know that you'll be escorting me to the Harvest Ball on Monday."

"I'll be the one in the blue dress," said Marleigh as she smiled and climbed the tree to her bedroom window as she had done so many times before. Marleigh pulled the window shut behind her and disappeared from sight.

Kip was alone, and the sky was bright, and the night air was warm as he walked home. He was in no hurry, and the streets were nearly empty. Come to think of it, they were completely empty. Before he knew why, the hair on his arms was standing on end, and he could hear his own heartbeat in the silence. The streetlights dimmed, sending a chill through Kip's body. He felt as if someone was watching him. The eerie feeling wrapped around him, and this time there was no fog.

Kip stood in silence for a moment and could hear his heart beating and the sound of his breath and something else. It was a raspy sound that sounded something like a dried leaf being dragged across stone and then back again. It was coming from the alleyway between Elijah Winstead's house and the bakery. Something was there watching him, and if it had been foggy that night, Kip might not have seen what was watching him. The air was clear that night, and the stars shone brightly, and Kip saw what was watching him. Something dark stood in the alleyway, and it was several feet taller than Kip and shaped like a man, but it wasn't a man. It was a shadow, and it spoke in a growl or maybe it sounded more like fingernails being dragged across a chalkboard. The words it spoke were slow and deliberate.

"Where is the book, Kip?" The voice echoed with a chilling resonance, sending shivers down Kip's spine.

Kip said nothing. The darkness crept closer, engulfing the alleyway.

"Where is the book... Kip?" The words slithered like tendrils of shadow, dripping with menace.

"I don't have it."

"Of course, you have it. I felt you take it," the voice growled, wrapping around Kip like a suffocating cloak.

Kip's heart pounded in his chest, but he forced himself to stand firm. "What did you do to Gary?"

"What did I do to Gary, you ask? I did what you wanted, Kip." The shadow's voice grew louder.

"What I wanted? I didn't want anything to happen to him!" Kip protested.

"Oh, but you did want this. Now bring me the book before you lose everyone!" The darkness swirled menacingly around the shadow, its form distorting and growing. "Bring me the book, Kip, or they will all be shadows, and I will pry it from your fingers!"

The voice reverberated through the empty town, each word dripping with malice. Then, as suddenly as it had appeared, the darkness faded into the night, leaving Kip alone in the chilling silence. Sweat coated his brow, and his hands trembled with fear. He knew he had to find the book, but he didn't know how.

~ 6 ~

WHERE SKIES
BECOME GRAY

Snow drifted through the open window, the white fluff dancing and twirling around the room before finding places to rest, accumulating in some spots and melting in others. The warm breeze from the night before had lured Kip into leaving the window open. Kip wouldn't have left the window open had he known there was a chance for snow. Neither Kip nor the town of Arno had seen snow for many years before that day.

The town was wrapped in a blanket of white, with the snow continuing to fall lazily in the early morning light. The streets, pumpkins, and hay bales were all covered. Snow piled up against the general store that Kip called home, completely covering the second-to-last step that hardly counted as a step at all. Snow had come to Arno, and no one found it odd but Kip.

Kip took to the stairs with bounds and leaps. Uncle John and Aunt Susan were having breakfast as Kip bolted past them. He flung the door open and ran into the street. The wind howled, and snow whirled around him; it was cold and incredible. Kip had never seen, nor had he ever felt anything like it.

The stalls and booths from the day before were all covered in white, and the townsfolk were out and about as if it were any other day. The squablins were also out and quickly showed their displeasure with the white intruders falling from the sky. They ran amok through the town, biting and snapping at the snow as it fell. Kip watched one squablin nuzzle close to the ground much like a cat preparing to pounce on a mouse. Its eyes widened as it found its target, and the fuzzy creature bounded into the air after it. Kip couldn't help but laugh as the squablin landed and sunk into the snow, leaving only a bushy tail visible.

"Hey, Kip Carringer!" shouted Marleigh.

The sound of Marleigh's voice put a smile on Kip's face, and he was smiling as he began to turn towards her. Kip shouldn't have been smiling because a fluffy white projectile was headed towards his face, all part of her seemingly masterful plan to hit Kip in the face with a snowball. The plan obviously worked, and it was a direct hit. Kip tried to return fire, but the snowball he made was inferior and fell apart before finding its mark.

"You're not very good at this," Marleigh remarked, her voice teasing.

"I've never thrown a snowball before!" Kip defended himself.

"Excuses won't make you any better, Kip Carringer. I

had to wait out here for nearly an hour for you to come outside! That's called dedication."

"Well, I'm glad your dedication paid off," Kip chuckled.

"Me too," said Marleigh, flashing her usual grin. "Is this your doing? I think I'm starting to catch on to all this book stuff."

"Yes... all I did was write about snow. I wasn't expecting this to happen."

"Something else happened too, come on." Marleigh's expression faded, replaced by concern as she motioned for Kip to follow her.

Kip followed Marleigh to the source of her worry. Before long, they were standing in front of Mr. Winstead's house. Shadows stretched out and twined around the little brick house, and it wasn't just the house. The bakery was engulfed in darkness as well, and threads of black wove around the building and in and out of the windows. The darkness pulsed and writhed as it consumed.

"Gary's house is like this too," Marleigh noted.

"I saw it last night," said Kip.

"You saw this?"

"No, I saw the shadow monster."

"Kip Carringer, do we need to take you to the doctor?" Marleigh asked with concern.

"No, I'm serious. It was real, and it told me this was my fault."

"How is this your fault?"

"Because I wrote in that stupid book that I wanted Gary to leave me alone. I didn't mean for any of this to happen!" exclaimed Kip, his frustration evident.

"I know you didn't. We need to find that book; maybe we can figure out how to fix this."

Kip had only heard his Aunt Susan yell at him a few times before, and this time the whole town heard her. Of course, Kip turned red when she did, which made him stand out even more against the snowy backdrop.

"Kip Carringer, you get back in this house and get some warmer clothes on this instant!" Aunt Susan's voice echoed throughout the town, and Kip wondered if the shadow monster would be scared if she were yelling at it. They were both equally intimidating.

Marleigh followed Kip to the general store, where Kip went upstairs and donned a sweater and a second pair of pants. Tufts of snow were still scattered here and there in his room, and the teddy bear with the googly eyes was damp, one eye looking left and the other looking right.

Downstairs, Aunt Susan had prepared breakfast for Kip and Marleigh, while Uncle John read the paper as usual. They engaged in small talk about the festival and the play, laughing as they revisited the events of the night before.

"Kip, set this out for Melinda May," Aunt Susan instructed, handing Kip a saucer with a soup bowl filled with warm broth and noodles.

"Who is Melinda May?" Kip inquired.

"The sweet little squablin that hangs out around the back step. She likes her new name, and I made her a little bandanna to wear around her neck, but she ate it. A decision she's probably regretting right about now considering how cold it is outside."

Kip took the bowl, looking more confused than ever. He

couldn't think of a response, so he shrugged and walked to the back door. Brushing the snow off the back step, he set the bowl down and then waited.

Melinda May was accustomed to being fed there and was just around the corner. Her ears perked up as she looked at Kip carefully. Once she deemed him not a threat, the squablin went for the soup. Her little paws grasped the bowl, and she turned it up, slurping the broth and noodles in a flash. Then, taking a bite of the bowl, she dropped it in the snow before retreating back around the corner.

Kip watched as the squablin took off down the alley, noticing the zigzag pattern of paw prints scattered in the alleyway. They were squablin prints, and in that moment, Kip knew how they could find the book. He called for Marleigh and showed her the prints. They took some time to observe them and followed them around the town. The paw prints led behind the general store and weaved in and out around a couple of houses. Then they crossed Elm Road and went through the town park and garden. The prints led across Main Street and through the playground and past the school. Eventually, they led east, outside of Arno.

Kip and Marleigh stood at the edge of town, surveying the prints. The snow was still falling, but the squablin tracks were clear, leading into the trees. "Into the woods we go...again," said Marleigh with an optimistic smile.

Little did they know, the darkness was spreading under the snow, violent and unseen.

❈ ❈ ❈

The world was nearly silent around them. Kip tried but couldn't remember a time when everything had been so quiet. The only noise was the soft crunch of snow as it gave way under their feet. The world was colored gray and white, and it was cold, very cold.

Well outside of town, Kip noticed two different kinds of animal prints. One of them belonged to a squablin, and he thought the other might have been made by a fox. He followed the squablin tracks as best he could, and he and Marleigh pressed on.

They had been walking for what felt like hours. The snow continued to fall around them, and they couldn't see very far in any direction. Kip wasn't all too familiar with the woods east of town. He had been that way before a few times with his Uncle John to go fishing at a little pond, but now it was snowing, and Kip didn't recognize anything around them.

Occasionally, the sun would sneak past the blanket of clouds, making the snow resemble glitter floating and twirling from the sky. Kip wondered how much farther it would be and if they would find the squablins at all. The steady snowfall made the tracks difficult to follow, and Kip felt like he was guessing at which direction they should go. Here and there, the tracks were easy to identify, but the tracks were nowhere to be seen where they were.

"I'm cold," Marleigh said as she pulled her heavy coat tighter around her body. Snowflakes clung to her black-framed glasses, and her bright green eyes weren't as vivid as they usually were. They looked pale, washed-out, like a favorite sweater that had been washed too many times.

"Me too," said Kip. "Maybe we should turn back. We'll find another way."

The two walked into the clearing of trees, and the wind blew harder. Marleigh shivered, her teeth chattered, and neither Marleigh nor Kip noticed the dull cracking sound from beneath them. In an instant, the ground gave way under their feet as the ice broke, and the frigid water splashed and churned. Kip desperately reached for Marleigh, but she was gone. Kip fell to his knees, reaching into the dark and cold water, frantically grabbing for something he couldn't find.

"Marleigh!" Kip shouted, and his voice echoed through the snow-covered forest.

Friendship has a way of sparking courage, and in that

moment, Kip was fearless. He plunged into the water; Marleigh was all that mattered. Holding onto the ice above, he went under. Seconds felt like hours, and in those seconds, he found what he was looking for. Marleigh's eyes were closed, and her blonde hair floated toward the ice above. Kip wrapped an arm around her and used every bit of strength he had left to heave her onto the bed of snow above the ice.

Her cheeks were a crimson red, and her lips were a soft blue. She wasn't breathing. Kip pressed his lips against hers and blew. He could feel her chest rising as he did. Trying to feel for a pulse, his hands were nearly frozen, and he couldn't feel anything. Kip remembered what Mr. Berringer had taught them during safety week. He pressed his lips against hers once more and blew.

Kip sat up and clasped his hands together, placing them on her chest. His arms were straight as he pushed hard and counted. On the sixth push, Marleigh coughed and vomited, mostly water. Kip had never been so relieved to see someone throw up. Her eyes opened, and she gasped for air. Her soaked blonde hair clung to her face, and Kip pushed it aside. Her pale green eyes stared up at him for a moment before closing again.

"I'll keep you safe, I promise," whispered Kip. He wrapped her up in his arms and did his best to stand. Uncertain of their direction or location, he could feel her chest rise and fall with each breath, and for the moment, that was all that mattered. Kip started walking, screaming for help as loudly as he could. His own voice began to waver, and he was cold—very cold.

After a dozen steps or so, he tripped over something, and they tumbled into the soft, inviting snow. Kip's body burned and ached, his clothes dripping wet. His eyes were heavy, but he had to get Marleigh to safety. He took her in his arms once again and got back to his feet, determined to find help. That's when he saw the creature in front of him.

A squablin stood a short distance in front of him, missing most of its left ear, with snow clinging to its bushy fur. Kip would have sworn it looked concerned. That squablin was Melinda May. She raised up, clicked, and motioned her paw as if she wanted Kip to follow. Kip complied.

Time blurred for Kip, his body numb. He wasn't sure how long he followed Melinda May or how far he carried Marleigh. Kip only knew that she was breathing, and that gave him comfort and the strength to keep moving. The dumpy little creature he followed moved, for the most part, with grace through the trees and snow. Occasionally, the squablin would topple over and roll a few paces, becoming covered in snow. Melinda May didn't seem too fond of the snow; she would shake and shudder like a shaggy, wet dog, sending snow and ice careening in every direction.

When they reached a thick grouping of trees, the squablin stopped and examined Kip and Marleigh once more. She cocked her head to one side, eyeing them as if considering or contemplating something very important. Seemingly satisfied, she clicked and chattered a sound of approval and went to work moving and clearing a patch of dense brush. When she was done, the squablin pointed at a small opening that led through the underbrush. Kip couldn't see what was on the other side of the opening, and he did not want to set Marleigh down in the snow. His options were limited, so he laid her down gently, wrapped his arms around her chest, and began to pull her through the opening in the brush.

Kip emerged on the other side to find himself in a little shanty town. Small huts and makeshift shelters were scattered around, some built from twigs and discarded materials leaned against each other, while others were more complete. In the center of the town sat the remnants of a large pumpkin cart, turned upside down, with an opening crudely chewed out of one side and a little lean-to built from another side.

The cobbled settlement was nestled against a rock face on one end and completely surrounded by trees. The thick canopy above kept nearly all of the snow out, making it warm within the confines of that little area. Relief and a hint of disbelief washed over Kip as the squablins surrounded and pressed in close. Dozens of them vibrated and chirped to one another in the most disorderly fashion.

Melinda May skittered off into one of the makeshift homes and came back out dragging a wooden box. Climbing atop the box, she proceeded to bounce up and down, making an awful racket. The other squablins listened attentively as she clicked, motioned, and pointed. After a moment, they all turned back towards Kip and Marleigh. The littlest of the squablins reached out and took Kip's hand, tugging him gently.

Guided by the squablin, Kip entered the upside-down

pumpkin cart where there wasn't much room inside, but it was warm, with quilts and blankets piled around. Kip wrapped the quilts around Marleigh and laid down next to her. The littlest squablin climbed in between them and nestled in close. Two more squablins made their way in, followed by Melinda May. They squeezed in tight, cuddling and snuggling next to and on top of Kip and Marleigh.

Kip was warm, and he could once again feel his fingers and toes. The littlest squablin rested on his chest, its fur tickling his face. Kip's eyes grew heavy, and before long, they shut.

He slept, and he dreamt of snow, ice, and darkness. He plunged into the icy water, hearing Marleigh call his name, but she was nowhere to be found. A shadow lurked beneath the water's surface, its eyes void of color, staring at him. Kip could hear the darkness breathe and whisper his name, its black tendrils wrapping around his legs and chest, pulling him deeper into the abyss.

The darkness spoke words in his mind, unintelligible yet understood by Kip. "They are all shadows, Kip. Bring me what is mine," it breathed and rattled, the words echoing in his mind as he struggled to breathe under the dark waters.

In a flash, Kip's body jerked awake. He could feel the soft and comforting rumble of the littlest squablin as it purred and snored beside him. Marleigh snored softly beside him too. Another squablin had entered the room, watching him with curious orange eyes. Kip wondered how long it had been observing him. The squablin held something dark in its paws, which it pushed forward. Kip managed to free himself from the sleeping squablins without waking even one, not even Melinda May.

Kip picked up the book. It was engulfed in a shadowy haze, black tendrils pulsing and curling around the cover and through the pages. As Kip opened it, the darkness rose and fell. He glanced at the squablin.

"Thank you."

The squablin grabbed the cuff of Kip's trousers, pulling harder when Kip didn't move. Taking the hint, Kip followed after the squablin. It led him across the shanty town to a small lean-to home, where a thick quilt hung over an opening serving as a door.

Pushing the quilt aside, Kip peered inside. Two squablins lay motionless, curled up next to each other in the corner of the little hut. Their ears were laid back, their eyes shut tight, and a shadow clung to them, as if they had been dipped in black ink or crude oil. The inky blackness coated their fur and sloshed over their little bodies.

Kip's eyes burned as he tried to hold back tears, letting the quilt fall back in place. Turning around, he found Marleigh standing behind him, holding Melinda May. The squablin's tail was black, darkness creeping over her fur. Tears streaked Marleigh's face as the squablin's eyes began to close, her ears laid back, and she went still.

Marleigh knelt down, gently setting Melinda May in the little hut next to the other two squablins. Tears spilled down her face, hands trembling as she rubbed them away, the quilt closing shut once more.

"I'm going to kill that shadow if it's the last thing I do," she declared, fists clenched, anger resonating through her body. "Give me the book."

Flipping through the pages, Marleigh muttered to

herself, the squablins gathering around them. She paused when she found something, running her finger beneath the words as she read aloud, searching for something useful. When she found it, she read the words again, her eyes widening. There was a drawing on the page, and when she showed it to Kip, he struggled to make out the image. But Marleigh could see it clearly—a drawing of a monster made of shadows.

Within these pages resides a darkness, and if it ever escapes, it must never recover this book. With the book, it will have life, and the darkness will reign once again. I have protected this book for years and years, and I fear one day it will bring about my demise. Finally finding a home in Arno, away from my sisters, I have found peace. I hope they are well and safe, and I miss them dearly.
-Lady Magdalene

The day began to fade, and little by little, twilight stole the light that had filtered through the trees above. Inside the squablin town, it was growing darker, and night would soon fall.

"Does it say anything about how to stop the shadow?" asked Kip.

"I don't know. It's getting harder to read, and I can barely see anything."

"We need to head back to town. Everyone will be looking for us," said Kip. "I didn't realize we slept that long."

"We can figure this out when we get home," she paused. "Do we know how to get home?"

"No, but they do."

The squablins had gathered around them; there were at least two or three dozen of them. The littlest squablin pressed out of the pack and climbed onto Kip, coming to rest on his shoulder. The squablin clicked and pointed to its little paw.

Marleigh scratched behind the squablin's ear. "I think this one knows the way. I'm going to call you, Miss Snuggles."

The squablin growled at her and flashed its teeth.

"Mr. Snuggles?" she asked, and the squablin nodded and purred. "Mr. Snuggles it is then."

They worked their way through the little opening and outside of the shanty town. Kip made sure to cover the entrance back, using sticks and brush to do so. Satisfied, they headed back towards Arno. Snow continued to fall and gather on the forest floor, but it was softer now than it had been earlier. The sun had completely set, and the moonlight splashed down into the trees, turning the black of night into a pale gray. At least they were dry and as warm as could be. The squablins brought them pies, blankets, and quilts before they left. Kip and Marleigh both declined the pie, but they graciously accepted the warmth of the blankets. They were exhausted—well, Kip and Marleigh were exhausted. Mr. Snuggles rode on Kip's shoulder, occasionally jumping down to sniff the ground or to look around. Once, he jumped off to relieve himself on a bush.

The moon was high in the night sky when they heard the shouts and caught a glimpse of a soft, wavering glow in the distance. The glow was from a lantern, and the shouting was from nearly the entire population of Arno. They had come looking for Kip and Marleigh. There were very few words spoken that night, just waves of relief, warm embraces, and a lot of tears. Kip wasn't sure if Aunt Susan was ever going to let him go. She held him, squeezed him, and every time she began to let go, she would grab him again and hold him tighter. That was also the first time Marleigh had ever seen her dad cry. Mr. Belle sobbed and picked her up, carrying her the rest of the way home like he had when she was a little girl.

Uncle John cradled Kip and carried him home as well. Kip never realized how strong his uncle was or just how much his aunt and uncle cared for him until that night. After that night, he knew very well. Last but not least, Mr. Snuggles also hitched a ride home. He was buried deep in Aunt Susan's jacket and wrapped up in her arms. Kip told Aunt Susan about Melinda May, and she wept and told him that everything would be alright. She said that Melinda May just had the shadow, and that she was strong and would make it through. Kip told her it was all his fault, and that he was sorry. Kip didn't remember Uncle John putting him in bed that night, but that is where he ended up and where he slept. When he slept, he dreamed about the shadow and the darkness, about Melinda May and the other squablins, about Gary Turner, and about the shadow monster and the book.

~ 7 ~

WHERE ALL HOPE IS LOST AND COURAGE MATTERS

Kip awoke to the sounds of birds mooing, and the late morning sunlight that streamed into his room. He jumped out of bed, sending his blankets flying, along with Mr. Snuggles. The squablin, who had been curled up at his feet, tumbled onto the floor and growled at Kip before scurrying downstairs.

Realizing he was running late, Kip hurriedly dressed, opting for the nearest pair of pants and a sweater. He ran his fingers through his shaggy brown hair, still a bit too long. The book sat on his desk, still shrouded in shadows. Snatching it up, he stuffed it into his bag, accidentally knocking over the teddy bear with the googly eyes in the process.

Rushing downstairs, Kip was greeted with even more hugs than the night before.

"Don't you ever scare me like that again!" exclaimed Aunt Susan.

"I promise I won't," replied Kip.

"Good! Now have some breakfast." She pulled out a chair for him. Mr. Snuggles was in the next chair over, already eating his breakfast. The squablin had a pancake still hanging out of his mouth, with syrup matted all in his fur.

"But I'm late for school!" pleaded Kip.

"School will have to wait," said Uncle John, his attention on the newspaper. "It's going to be alright if you're late just this once."

"Is Marleigh alright?" asked Kip.

"Yes, she's fine," replied Uncle John. "I ran into Mr. Belle when I went out for the paper, and he said she was still sleeping."

Kip was relieved to hear it. His muscles were still sore from the day before, and the whole adventure had taken a toll on his body. He was worried about Marleigh. Kip thought about telling Uncle John and Aunt Susan about falling in the ice. He considered telling them about the book too, but he didn't want to make them worry, deciding it would be best if he didn't tell them the entire story.

After breakfast, Kip hugged Aunt Susan and kissed her on the cheek, then hugged Uncle John. Aunt Susan picked up Mr. Snuggles and told him it was time for a bath. His ears perked up, and there was a look of sheer terror on the littlest squablin's face.

The snow continued to fall, and it remained cold. The town was nearly silent, and the streets were mostly empty. Kip cut through the town park and garden on his way to Marleigh's house, finding snow-covered pumpkins and cornstalks leaning this way and that way under the weight of the fresh snow. He also found Daisy Appleton sitting on a little wooden bench, a shadow of her former self. Her eyes were drawn shut, and she was curled up motionless on the bench, covered in darkness like Gary Turner, the two squablins in the hut, and Melinda May. Kip missed her laugh and wondered where Calvin O'Neal was.

A little farther on, Kip could see the quaint brick house a couple of dozen paces off Main Street. Smoke curled into the late morning air from the chimney as he turned off from Elm Road. Marleigh was bundled in a heavy coat, sitting on her front step.

"You're late too?" asked Kip.

"Yeah, looks that way. I figured I would wait for you."

"Well, I'm glad you did. I brought the book so you can finish reading it at school, and hopefully, we can fix this."

"So, what are we waiting for?" Marleigh grinned her usual grin, and the two headed off toward school.

✱ ✱ ✱

The hallways were silent, and their footsteps echoed and bounced off the brick walls as the heavy doors slammed behind them.

"Something isn't right," said Marleigh.

They walked down the hall and toward Mr. Tinson's class. Mr. Tinson was at his desk, frozen in black. Shadows swirled around him, sloshing and pouring out around his desk. Jeremy Rider and Betty Clairmont were the only students in the classroom. They were shadows too.

Kip and Marleigh ran from room to room and found only shadows. Well, almost only shadows; Mr. Braverman was in his classroom, drawing the periodic table on his chalkboard. He was very serious about such things, and it was doubtful that he would ever even notice that he had no students to teach.

Back in the hall, they heard a noise. A noise that was becoming all too familiar to Kip. It was a raspy sound that sounded something like a dried leaf being dragged across stone and then back again. Marleigh was about to call out to it, but Kip stopped her and put a hand over her mouth.

"Where's the book, Kip?" The voice was hoarse and scratchy.

Kip pulled Marleigh close and whispered into her ear, "It's the shadow monster."

Her eyes widened, and she did her best to peek around the corner without being noticed. She watched as the shadow walked down the hall. With every passing step, darkness bled into the floor and drenched the walls. Shadows dripped from the ceiling and splashed down into the black below.

"I know you're here, Kip. I watched you come in, and I felt the book. Marleigh is here too, isn't she, Kip?" The shadow's voice, low and ominous, reverberated through the empty halls like a chilling wind. Pausing, it let out a menacing roar that seemed to freeze the very air. "Hand over the book!"

Kip grabbed Marleigh by the arm and hurried her down the hall. They quickly turned and slipped into the gymnasium. Inside, tables were set up with banners and streamers hanging here and there. It was Monday, and they were supposed to attend the Harvest Ball that evening. Instead, they found themselves being pursued by a shadow.

Hiding behind the bleachers, Kip retrieved the book from his bag and handed it to Marleigh. She began to skim through the pages as they spoke in hushed tones.

"Most of this is just gibberish," she said. "I don't get it."

"Does it mention anything else about the shadow monster?" asked Kip, his voice barely above a whisper.

"That's what I'm looking for."

The slamming of doors and the shadow's ominous screams echoed through the halls, growing louder and closer with each passing moment.

For if the monster inside gets the book, it will become whole and it will devour this world as it has done with others before.
-Lady Magdalene

"How can something devour an entire world!?" exclaimed Kip.

"I don't know, but it's turning this town into a shadow. What do we do?" she asked.

"We need to get out of here and leave Arno. We'll find some answers, but we can't do it here. Maybe there's something in the witch's house that can help us."

The doors to the gym burst open, and darkness sloshed inside. The banners and streamers were left haphazardly hanging, and tables overturned.

"They are all shadows, Kip. Now give it to me, or I will

swallow this town whole!" As the monster howled and wailed, the gym started to shake, and the bleachers began to shift, and black ink trickled down between the seats.

"We have to go. Follow me." Kip took Marleigh's hand, and they ran towards the door.

The shadows pulsed and writhed under their feet, while the monster roared and flailed after them. Kip and Marleigh sprinted down the hallway and pushed through the doors. They stepped out into the snow, and the world around them was enveloped in darkness.

The town was being consumed by shadows, and darkness spilled from the sky. There was no sun, no stars, and no moon. There was just darkness. The lamps lining the street were the only source of light. Kip and Marleigh ran down First Street until they reached Main Street.

"I have to check on my dad and make sure he's okay," said Marleigh.

"I have to check on Uncle John and Aunt Susan. Stay at home, and I'll meet you there," replied Kip.

"Be careful, Kip," Marleigh cautioned.

"Just don't leave, I'll be right back after I find Uncle John and Aunt Susan. Maybe we can all make a run for it," Kip reassured her.

Marleigh nodded and took off toward her house. Kip watched until she closed the door and then headed across town. Everything was covered in black, even the snowflakes falling from the sky. The general store was etched in shadows, and the only light came from the lantern hanging by the front door.

Kip shouted for his uncle and aunt as he climbed the

steps, making sure to avoid the second from the bottom step that hardly counted as a step at all. He threw the door open and shouted again, but there wasn't much reason to shout. Uncle John was slumped over in his chair, still holding the morning newspaper. Aunt Susan lay by the stove in the back, with Mr. Snuggles sitting in front of her like a well-trained guard dog. None of them heard Kip's shouts, and none of them moved. They were all shadows, and darkness lolled and sloshed over their bodies.

Kip fell to his knees, his eyes burning with anger. The shadow had taken everything from him. Well, almost everything; he wouldn't let the monster take everything. Standing up, he wiped away the tears and rushed upstairs. Kip sheathed the broadsword from the corner and slung it over his shoulder. He gathered a few belongings and returned downstairs. He wished Aunt Susan would be there, her arms open, waiting to embrace him, but she wasn't. She was a shadow, and he was alone.

Stuffing a loaf of bread, a jar of jam, and a few other items in his bag, he left. He ran as fast as he could, cutting through the town park and garden, trying his best to avoid the encroaching darkness. However, Kip should have taken a different route because that's where the monster was waiting for him.

"I am tiring of these games, Kip. Give me the book!"

"You can't have it!" shouted Kip.

The shadow paused for a moment and looked Kip up and down. There was a wooden bench and several rows of pumpkins between them, and the monster still towered over Kip.

"Where's Marleigh, Kip? Maybe she'll give me the book."

"You leave her alone!" Kip shouted as he pulled the jar of jam from his bag. He heaved it with all his strength toward the shadow monster. The jar missed and shattered against a nearby tree.

The monster's laughter echoed through the eerie silence. It reveled in Kip's futile attempt, its voice dripping with sinister glee, but Kip wasn't trying to hit the monster. At least that's how it would be told later. More than likely, Kip intended on hitting the monster with the jam and just missed, but when he missed and the monster watched the jam soar off course, Kip saw an opportunity to escape.

When the monster stopped laughing and regained its composure, it spoke and said, "You can't hurt me, Kip. I'm just a shadow without the book. Nothing can harm a shadow." But when the monster looked up, Kip was gone.

Kip was already hiding in the darkness of the alleyway between Mr. Winstead's house and the bakery. The shadow monster thrashed in fury when it realized what had happened, and it began to hunt for Kip, who was already cutting through backyards on his way to Marleigh's house.

Kip eased the door open and found Mr. Belle first. Black waves crashed around him as he sat at the kitchen table reading the paper, similar to how he found his Uncle John. Kip whispered for Marleigh, but there was no response. He could still hear the shadow monster shouting outside as it scoured the streets of Arno looking for him and the book.

Kip stepped over markers and containers of glitter and

made his way upstairs. He had never seen Marleigh's room before, and he didn't really see it that day either. Black shadows leaked from the molding and covered the walls, the bed, and the little desk in the corner. He almost left, but then he saw a sliver of light under the closet door.

"Marleigh?" he whispered as he approached the door.

Kip opened it, and there she was, sitting in the closet with a lit candle.

"Hey, Kip Carringer." Her voice was weak and shaky.

"Got room for one more in there?" he asked.

"Sure," she said, trying to manage a smile.

Kip sat across from her in the little closet with the candle in between them. A thin line of what looked like black thread was winding up the candlestick, and the light wavered.

"Are your aunt and uncle okay?"

Kip shook his head and looked down.

"My dad..."

"I know," said Kip. "I'm sorry, Marleigh."

"It's not your fault."

Even though she said it wasn't his fault, Kip still felt like it was. They sat in the dimly lit closet, and Kip put his hand on top of Marleigh's hand, and he put the other inside his pocket. There was something inside his pocket. Kip pulled out a little crumpled slip of paper. He opened it carefully and smoothed out the creases. There was only one word written inside: Courage. Aunt Susan would often give him notes of encouragement and praise. Usually, they were longer than one word and would often say something like, "you'll do great today" or "have the best day at school" or "don't give up". This note only said "courage".

Love has a way of sparking courage, and in that moment, Kip was fearless. He stood up, and Marleigh gave him a confused look. They could hear the monster in a rage outside, wailing and screaming.

"I know what I have to do," Kip's voice was calm. "I have to give him the book."

"You can't! You know what the book says, that thing will destroy everything. We can't let this happen to everyone else."

"I won't let it happen to anyone else." Kip threw his arms around Marleigh's neck and hugged her tighter than he had ever hugged anyone. "I'll make sure nothing happens to you. Stay here."

The door closed, and he was gone, and the flame on

the candle danced for a moment longer until the shadow devoured it. Marleigh was alone, in the dark.

Kip ran into the street and held the book high.

"Come get your stupid book, you stupid shadow!"

The shadow emerged from the ground a dozen paces or so in front of him. Black ink trickled and splashed around him. Everything was covered in darkness, and the light from the streetlamps was barely visible.

"Good boy. Now hand it to me."

"Take it!" shouted Kip as he threw the book to the shadow monster.

The monster had no face, but it smiled and grinned as it wrapped its black fingers around the leather binding of the old book. The pages began to crumble into ash, spinning and swirling around the monster. When the pages were nothing but dust, the binding turned to ash as well, covering the towering beast.

Kip watched as its skeleton materialized and the monster began to take a definite shape. He watched sinew form and attach bone to bone and muscle to bone. He watched veins lace through its body and become engorged with blood. He also watched the monster's heart as it formed and began to beat and pump, and in that moment, Kip drew his sword.

He raced cautiously toward the shadow that wasn't entirely a shadow. He calculated each step so that he didn't slip in the darkness and snow under his feet. He screamed as he lifted the sword and plunged it deep into the chest of the monster. The sword ripped through forming flesh and cut through the heart of the beast.

The shadow monster howled in pain, jerking violently as its body crumpled to the ground with the sword still buried deep in its chest.

"This can't be," it uttered with terror, pain, and agony in its voice, sounding more like a man than a shadow.

The darkness quivered and pulsed all around them, and light concentrated around the monster. A low, painful hum rang out as the light intensified. Suddenly, the light exploded, taking the shadow monster with it. Kip was sent reeling through the air, landing on his back with a hard thud. The world began to spin, and his vision faded to black.

~ 8 ~

WHERE BIRDS CHIRP

Marleigh's voice was soft, and Kip opened his eyes to find her mere inches from his face. "Wake up, sleepyhead. We're gonna be late... and you need to change your clothes."

The sun had begun to set over the horizon, casting shades of gold and red throughout the sky. The air was warm, and Kip found himself lying sprawled out in a patch of lush green grass. He wondered why it was so warm, and then he wondered why he was outside. Marleigh took his hand in hers and helped pull him to his feet.

"What happened?" asked Kip.

"Oh, not much," replied Marleigh. "You just killed a shadow monster and saved the whole town."

There were no words, and Kip didn't know what to say.

"Are you ready?" she asked.

"Ready for what?"

"The Harvest Ball, silly," she paused for a moment. "Maybe it's the summer ball now. I don't know."

"What day is it?"

"It's still Monday, Kip Carringer," Marleigh replied.

"Why was I sleeping in the grass?"

"Not sure, but you looked so cozy I just left you there. Now let's go get you changed. You're filthy, and that just won't do."

They began to walk towards the general store when Kip stopped, and Marleigh made it a few paces before she stopped and gave him a puzzled look. Kip gazed toward the streetlamp. A pale grey bird sat atop the light preening its feathers. The bird whistled and chirped as it worked.

"That bird is chirping!?" Kip exclaimed.

"Birds chirp, Kip. Get used to it." A sly smile crept onto her lips as she winked at him and spun back around. "I guess everything is back to normal since the book is gone. Now hurry up, we're going to be late!"

They were both caught off guard when they heard the shouts erupt and the loud crack of a broom hitting something. Melinda May came sprinting around the corner, her face covered in pie and looking quite pleased with herself. Mrs. Tubbertown, wearing her nightgown and curlers, was in pursuit after Melinda May. Two more squablins came barreling out of the front door, and a very winded Mrs. Tubbertown soon gave up.

Marleigh's face lit up with delight, and so did Kip's, and they both looked at each other and smiled and shouted one word. "Squablins!"

"But how are they still here?" questioned Kip. "The book is gone."

Marleigh grinned and pulled out a worn and tattered

piece of paper from her back pocket. She unfolded the paper and showed it to Kip. It was the page from the book where Kip had drawn the squablin.

"I ripped the page out," she said. "I didn't know what would happen to them if we destroyed the book, and I didn't want them to go away."

"Me either," said Kip.

❋ ❋ ❋

The gym was dimly lit, with paper lamps suspended from the ceiling with twine. Lively music filled the air, and tables were adorned with punch, snacks, and treats. A warm breeze drifted in through the open doors.

Uncle John and Mr. Belle sat side by side in the bleachers, engrossed in their newspapers as usual. Aunt Susan served punch, with Mr. Snuggles curled up on her feet, holding a sandwich in his little paws. He wore a plaid bandana and appeared quite content.

Calvin O'Neal and Daisy Appleton danced together, wrapped in each other's arms. Daisy waved and smiled warmly at Kip when she spotted him, while Calvin nodded in acknowledgment.

"Hey Kippy," Gary Turner stepped up next to Kip and placed a hand on his shoulder. "Guess you're really the hero of Arno after all. What you did was pretty cool."

"Thanks, Gary."

"Maybe you should come by one day after school, and we can hang out like we used to. I think I still have those tin foil swords in the closet."

"Sounds fun." Gary Turner smiled and patted Kip on the back.

As the music slowed and the crowd thinned, Marleigh stood in the center of the gym. She wore a pale blue dress, with a lily tucked behind her ear. Her blonde hair was loosely tied with a bow, and her hands were clasped behind her back.

"Kip Carringer, don't tell me you're going to make a princess lead herself in a dance."

"No," he replied. "I think the hero should lead this one." Kip took Marleigh's hand, and they danced, laughed, and had a happily ever after.

~The End~

EPILOGUE

When she smiled, the creases around her lips and the wrinkles on her cheeks revealed her many years of life. Lady Schala knelt over the freshly turned dirt and gently laid a golden sunflower on the mound.

"May you sleep soundly, sister," Lady Schala's voice was calm and sweet, like that of a mother comforting a child.

"She always did love sunflowers," Lady Alma's voice was shaky, and she had the hood of her tunic drawn tightly to hide the tears that streaked her weathered face.

"I just knew we shouldn't have left Magdalene alone with that book," said Lady Elaine as she leaned against the grand willow tree. Her gaze fell toward the hillside in the west and the setting summer sun.

"Now sister, Magdalene was wise, and she knew how to take care of herself. There's nothing we could have done. This was the work of fate," said Lady Margaret as she slid an acorn into her coat pocket. Tiny paws reached out and claimed it. The squablin nestled back into the bottom of her pocket and went to work trying to open the treat as Lady Margaret scratched behind its ears.

"You're so sure it was fate that did this, are you?" another sister asked with a raised brow.

"Hush," interjected Lady Schala. "The whole lot of you need to hush. We haven't seen each other in ages, and we're here to bury our sister." She looked around at her sisters, who were all looking anywhere other than where Lady Schala's eyes were. "Where is Ophelia?"

"Last I heard, she was still in the city," replied Lady Elaine.

"And the sword?"

"With her, I presume."

About the Author

Kyle Bagsby is a dedicated educator, loving husband, and proud father of three boys. Residing in Middle Tennessee, Kyle balances his roles as a classroom teacher and a writer, drawing inspiration from his experiences and adventures with his family.

Kyle's journey as an author began with his head buried in a book as a child, sparking a lifelong love for storytelling. He went on to study Elementary Education where his passion for writing grew. Specializing in middle-grade fantasy, he crafts stories that captivate and inspire young readers.

Thank you for joining in on this exciting journey!

www.ingramcontent.com/pod-product-compliance
Lightning Source LLC
Chambersburg PA
CBHW021555150726
47990CB00006B/2554